Heather stared at Court, seeing the forbidding frown that drew his thick black brows together, and felt her breath hitch in her throat. He looked positively murderous.

Yet, even with that chilling expression on his face, there was no question in her mind that Court was one of the most magnetic and compelling men she had ever encountered. Despite her fear of him, of the situation, she found herself drawn to him like a moth to a flame.

Even as she tried to will herself into indifference, her fingers twitched with the desire to test the texture of his ebony hair. Her lips tingled, as though anticipating the touch of his full, sensual mouth. But his eyes… His golden predator's eyes were the most mesmerizing thing about him.

She swallowed, wondering if maybe, just maybe, she was in worse trouble than she had ever imagined….

Dear Reader,

Once again, Silhouette Intimate Moments has rounded up six top-notch romances for your reading pleasure, starting with the finale of Ruth Langan's fabulous new trilogy. *The Wildes of Wyoming—Ace* takes the last of the Wilde men and matches him with a pool-playing spitfire who turns out to be just the right woman to fill his bed—and his heart.

Linda Turner, a perennial reader favorite, continues THOSE MARRYING McBRIDES! with *The Best Man*, the story of sister Merry McBride's discovery that love is not always found where you expect it. Award-winning Ruth Wind's *Beautiful Stranger* features a heroine who was once an ugly duckling but is now the swan who wins the heart of a rugged "prince." Readers have been enjoying Sally Tyler Hayes' suspenseful tales of the men and women of DIVISION ONE, and *Her Secret Guardian* will not disappoint in its complex plot and emotional power. Christine Michels takes readers *Undercover with the Enemy*, and Vickie Taylor presents *The Lawman's Last Stand*, to round out this month's wonderful reading choices.

And don't miss a single Intimate Moments novel for the next three months, when the line takes center stage as part of the Silhouette 20th Anniversary celebration. Sharon Sala leads off A YEAR OF LOVING DANGEROUSLY, a new in-line continuity, in July; August brings the long-awaited reappearance of Linda Howard—and hero Chance Mackenzie—in *A Game of Chance;* and in September we reprise 36 HOURS, our successful freestanding continuity, in the Intimate Moments line. And that's only a small taste of what lies ahead, so be here this month and every month, when Silhouette Intimate Moments proves that love and excitement go best when they're hand in hand.

Leslie J. Wainger
Executive Senior Editor

Please address questions and book requests to:
Silhouette Reader Service
U.S.: 3010 Walden Ave., P.O. Box 1325, Buffalo, NY 14269
Canadian: P.O. Box 609, Fort Erie, Ont. L2A 5X3

UNDERCOVER
WITH THE ENEMY
CHRISTINE MICHELS

Silhouette®
INTIMATE™MOMENTS®
Published by Silhouette Books
America's Publisher of Contemporary Romance

Dedicated to the memory of my nephew,
Justine Stanley Byrt. July 3, 1985 to June 18, 1999.
You left us much too soon, Justin. We'll miss you.

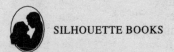 SILHOUETTE BOOKS

ISBN 0-373-27083-6

UNDERCOVER WITH THE ENEMY

Copyright © 2000 by Sharry C. Michels

All rights reserved. Except for use in any review, the reproduction or utilization of this work in whole or in part in any form by any electronic, mechanical or other means, now known or hereafter invented, including xerography, photocopying and recording, or in any information storage or retrieval system, is forbidden without the written permission of the editorial office, Silhouette Books, 300 East 42nd Street, New York, NY 10017 U.S.A.

All characters in this book have no existence outside the imagination of the author and have no relation whatsoever to anyone bearing the same name or names. They are not even distantly inspired by any individual known or unknown to the author, and all incidents are pure invention.

This edition published by arrangement with Harlequin Books S.A.

® and TM are trademarks of Harlequin Books S.A., used under license. Trademarks indicated with ® are registered in the United States Patent and Trademark Office, the Canadian Trade Marks Office and in other countries.

Visit Silhouette at www.eHarlequin.com

Printed in U.S.A.

Books by Christine Michels

Silhouette Intimate Moments

A Season of Miracles #900
Undercover with the Enemy #1013

CHRISTINE MICHELS

is a chronic daydreamer with a vivid imagination. Since her day job as an accountant provided little outlet for her creative inclinations (creative accounting being frowned upon in professional circles), Christine turned to writing. She is now an award-winning author of futuristic, historical and contemporary romances. Christine lives in Alberta with her husband of over twenty years, their teenage son and a small menagerie of pets, consisting of a finicky Pomeranian, two imperious cats and a hedgehog with a prickly personality.

IT'S OUR 20th ANNIVERSARY!
We'll be celebrating all year,
Continuing with these fabulous titles,
On sale in June 2000.

Romance

#1450 Cinderella's Midnight Kiss
Dixie Browning

#1451 Promoted—To Wife!
Raye Morgan

AN OLDER MAN
#1452 Professor and the Nanny
Phyllis Halldorson

The *Circle K Sisters*
#1453 Never Let You Go
Judy Christenberry

The WEDDING AUCTION
#1454 Contractually His
Myrna Mackenzie

#1455 Just the Husband She Chose
Karen Rose Smith

Desire

MAN of the MONTH
#1297 Tough To Tame
Jackie Merritt

#1298 The Rancher and the Nanny
Caroline Cross

MATCHED IN MONTANA
#1299 The Cowboy Meets His Match
Meagan McKinney

#1300 Cheyenne Dad
Sheri WhiteFeather

The Baby Bank
#1301 The Baby Gift
Susan Crosby

#1302 The Determined Groom
Kate Little

Intimate Moments

 WILDES of WYOMING
#1009 The Wildes of Wyoming—Ace
Ruth Langan

Those Marrying McBrides!
#1010 The Best Man
Linda Turner

#1011 Beautiful Stranger
Ruth Wind

#1012 Her Secret Guardian
Sally Tyler Hayes

#1013 Undercover with the Enemy
Christine Michels

#1014 The Lawman's Last Stand
Vickie Taylor

Special Edition

#1327 The Baby Quilt
Christine Flynn

#1328 Irish Rebel
Nora Roberts

Baby Set
#1329 To a MacAllister Born
Joan Elliott Pickart

A Family Bond
#1330 A Man Apart
Ginna Gray

DESERT ROGUES
#1331 The Sheik's Secret Bride
Susan Mallery

#1332 The Price of Honor
Janis Reams Hudson

Chapter 1

"Take off your pants, Mr. Gabriele, and we'll get started." Heather glanced at the man she'd heard enter the room long enough to get an impression of dark handsomeness, but she didn't turn to face him. She couldn't. Not yet.

"What did you say?" Court Gabriele's response was low, scarcely above a murmur, and infinitely cold.

Heather prayed for courage. It's only that he'd expected more in the way of idle chitchat before getting down to business, she told herself. Please let that be all it was! "I said, take off your pants." She focused almost desperately on her own preparations. "I need to be able to see the functioning of the leg muscles while we work. You can put on a pair of exercise shorts, if you like. I have some with me if you don't have your own."

There was a second of silence. "Not so fast." The frostiness of his tone eradicated any hope she'd had that this might be easy. Court Gabriele's voice was deep and rich—Heather had always perceived color in sound, and his voice brought to mind a luxurious burgundy. But at the moment, it was burgundy on ice.

She wanted to run, to escape while she could.

But DiMona's words echoed in her mind once more, staying her with their sinister threat. *Get into Gabriele's house and find out what he's up to. As long as you don't hold out on me, your brother will be fine. You understand?*

Yes, she understood. Escape was out of the question. She swallowed, trying to dislodge the knot of terror that had been stuck in her throat for days. Somehow, she had to gird herself to face Mr. Court Gabriele. *You can do this, Heather,* she told herself for the millionth time. *You have to. For Des.* Her breath hitched and she sent a simple prayer winging heavenward. *God, help me.*

Slowly, she turned to meet for the first time the man she'd been sent to spy on. She was terrified that he'd perceive the duplicitous nature of her presence in her expression. Terrified that any associate of Rick DiMona's wouldn't think twice about killing her if it was in his own best interests. Terrified that she was going to screw up and her brother would pay the price—with his life.

She lifted her gaze to confront Gabriele and received a shock to her system that caused everything within her to go still. Her breath arrested in her throat. Her heart stuttered. And her eyes widened. Oh, no! She hadn't prepared herself for *this!*

Court Gabriele was one of the most intensely charismatic men she'd ever seen. Not handsome, but certainly compelling, he was fit and quite tall. Six feet, at least. He wore his midnight-black hair in a cut that just narrowly escaped being regulation military in its severity. A few soft waves that had escaped the clippers lay against the crown of his head as though longing to spring into life but not quite daring to defy the ruthlessness of the comb that had restrained them. The exacting style made the harsh masculine planes of Gabriele's face—the firm square jawline, high cheekbones and bold blade of a nose—even more prominent, as though sculpted with an artist's precision to imply admirable strength of character. A false implication no doubt, considering the identity of his associates.

Stop gawking, Heather, she told herself. So what if Court Gabriele looked entirely too fit and self-confident to be the desk-bound professional that she'd expected. The last thing she wanted, or *needed,* was to notice Court Gabriele's appeal. She needed all her wits about her. Any distraction could get her killed. Yet, despite what her conscious mind might dictate, her hormones had definitely taken notice.

She drew a breath and reached desperately for normalcy. "Is there a problem?" For the first time, she noticed that he seemed to be leaning heavily on his cane, and her prior lack of perception irritated her. So much for professionalism; the man's mere presence had blinded her to her first duty: to help a man who hurt. "Are you in pain?" she asked, gesturing to the cane. Somehow, the badge of infirmity seemed more at odds with Court Gabriele than anyone she'd ever encountered.

His eyes were chips of amber ice. "No. I am not in pain," he said, his words clipped and abrupt. "But, yes, there is definitely a problem."

Heather nodded and left the ball in his court, studying him more closely for clues to his character while she waited for him to elaborate. He wore light-beige dress slacks that, judging from the way they draped his leanly muscled hips, appeared to have been crafted from linen, or perhaps raw silk, and a maroon T-shirt that hugged the muscular contours of his torso like a second skin. A small cell phone protruded from the breast pocket of the T-shirt. The unusual ensemble made a statement of casual elegance, and yet few men could have carried off the combination. Somehow, on Court Gabriele, the T-shirt looked as though it had been specifically designed to be worn with suit trousers.

"Just what the hell are you doing here?" His tone remained quiet, almost conversational yet, to Heather's ears, threat was inherent. Gabriele studied her with the most arresting golden topaz eyes she'd ever seen. The eyes of a predator waiting for a false move.

Oh, Lord! What had she gotten herself into? She was in the lion's den. An aura of darkness and danger clung to Court like a cape.

She swallowed and forced herself to move forward to offer her hand in introduction. "Oh, I'm sorry. I thought you knew. My name is Heather Buchanan, Mr. Gabriele. The Rockford Clinic sent me.'' She had no idea how DiMona had secured her current position at the clinic, and she hadn't asked. She just hoped that when this was all over she would still have a job. Or, failing that, that she'd at least be able to return to her old position at the Northwest Hospital. ''I'm your physical therapist.''

''I know who you are,'' he said. ''Ernest relayed what you told him when you arrived.'' A spark of awareness raced through Heather as he accepted her hand, all but swallowing it in his own large, warm grasp. She stifled the sensation ruthlessly. ''That doesn't answer my question.''

Ernest would be the burly doorman who had shown her in. ''I'm afraid I don't understand, Mr. Gabriele. I was under the impression that you weren't content with the therapy available at the clinic and had requested a personal therapist to aid you with intensive therapy in the hope of achieving a speedy recovery.''

He scowled. ''I specifically requested a male therapist, Ms. Buchanan. I was expecting a man named Miguel.''

Heather stared at the forbidding frown that drew his thick black brows together and felt her breath hitch in her throat. He looked positively murderous. Well, maybe thunderous was a better description.

She hoped.

Yet, even with that chilling expression on his face, there was no question in her mind that Court Gabriele was one of the most magnetic and compelling men she had ever encountered. Despite her fear of him, of the situation, she found herself drawn to him like a moth to a flame. She just hoped she would emerge from the encounter in better shape than the moth. But even as she tried to will herself into indifference, her fingers twitched with the desire to test the texture of his ebony hair. Her lips tingled as though anticipating the touch of his full, sensual lips. And her pulse accelerated as she reluctantly acknowledged how sexy the whisker shadow lurking beneath the smooth-shaven tanned skin of his strong jawline truly was. Even the small diamond stud he wore in his left ear seemed to somehow magnify his dark attractiveness, and Heather had never before found a man who wore an earring attractive. But his eyes…his golden predator's eyes were the most mesmerizing thing about him.

She swallowed and couldn't help wondering if maybe, just maybe, she was in worse trouble than she had ever imagined.

"Ms. Buchanan!"

She started at the sharp tone of his voice, her gaze flying up to meet his. "Yes?"

"Why isn't Miguel here?"

"I'm sorry, Mr. Gabriele, I don't know. Perhaps the clinic administrator can tell you."

Gabriele's frown sharpened, if that was possible. "Well, you can just take yourself back out that door and tell your boss that he doesn't need to bother sending me anyone until he has a decent *male* therapist available."

"A *male*—" Heather broke off, staring at him in shock. Of all the possibilities for failure that she'd imagined, a sexist attitude had not been among of them.

"Mr. Gabriele, let me assure you that when it comes to physical therapy I am *as* accomplished, if not more so, than most of my male colleagues. I have a Masters degree in physical therapy, and I graduated among the top in my class. I've been working for years without any complaints from my clients. In addition, I am licensed in therapeutic massage and aromatherapy. However, if you prefer to languish around using a cane rather than hastening the healing process, you are perfectly welcome to do so." Turning away, she began to throw her supplies haphazardly back into her case...and hesitated.

Oh, Lord, what had she done? If the righteous indignation ploy didn't reassure him, she'd left herself no recourse. And, she *needed* to be here. Des's life depended on her presence here. On what she could find out. But now...

"Just a moment," Gabriele barked.

Heather's heart leapt in relief even as her palm itched to slam the lid of her case and escape. Court Gabriele terrified her on every level, from his cold arrogance to her own inexplicable physical response to him. But she could allow neither her temper nor her hormones to rule. So, keeping her expression carefully neutral, she slowly turned to face him.

He studied her for a moment. Finally he said, "Your capabilities and intelligence are not in question, Ms. Buchanan."

"Then what's the problem?"

He watched her in silence and with every passing second the knot in Heather's stomach drew tighter until she was certain that the tension alone would make her vomit. Finally he said, "My reasons are personal, Ms. Buchanan.'' Leaning slightly on his cane, Gabriele approached her, halting a scant three feet away. Even injured as he was, his was an imposing presence, and Heather would have liked nothing better than to run from his house and never return. ''All right, Ms. Buchanan. You've convinced me to give you a chance. Tell me what you know about my condition,'' Gabriele ordered in a hard tone.

Heather felt her heart stutter. Now, knowing she could not afford to make a mistake, she responded carefully. ''I was told to review your file in its entirety before coming, so I assume I know everything that you've told your therapist at the clinic.''

''And that would be?'' he prompted.

''I know that about two-and-a-half weeks ago you were run off the road, into a ravine by a hit-and-run driver, and that you were trapped in your car until a passing motorist noticed the vehicle. During the almost three hours that you waited for rescue, something pressed down on your groin area crushing the femoral nerve to your right leg as well as seriously restricting the circulation to the leg through your femoral artery and vein. With the exception of a minor concussion and your leg injury, you were unhurt. You're a lucky man.''

''I don't feel lucky.'' With a sharp nod, he indicated that she should continue. ''What's the prognosis?''

Heather weighed her words carefully. ''Depending on the extent of the nerve damage, it may take considerable time for the feeling to return to your leg—particularly if the nerves have to regrow from the spine. And there is no guarantee that sensation will ever return completely. On the positive side, however, it's probable that the muscular weakness could pass reasonably quickly if we can get the blood flow back to normal with a rigorous program of therapy.

"Is the leg still cold to the touch?" she asked.

He nodded. "Yes. In the thigh area."

"The circulation problem is the first thing we have to address. Exercise will get the blood flowing to the leg more quickly and, hopefully, should get that crushed artery and the muscles functioning normally again.

"Can you walk at all without the aid of a cane?"

Gabriele stared at her in silence. "What did my file say?"

Ignoring the tension in her stomach, Heather forced herself to meet his impassive golden-eyed gaze, to match him look for look. "I believe it said that you could walk, but not reliably. That if you fail to keep the knee in a locked position, your leg can collapse without warning. Is that correct?"

"That's about right."

"May I ask you a question, Mr. Gabriele?"

He nodded, studying her with an inscrutable expression.

"Well…I was just wondering why you hadn't used your cell phone to call for help."

His lips twisted briefly in a wry expression. "Because, foolishly, I had forgotten to charge the battery."

"How unfortunate."

"Yes." Gabriele's gaze dropped to her throat, to

the exact spot where Heather could feel her pulse pounding. "Do I make you uncomfortable, Ms. Buchanan?"

What did the man want from her? But, if he could see her anxiety there was no sense in lying about it. "Yes, Mr. Gabriele, you do."

He studied her with a penetrating expression. "Why?"

Oh, Lord. She understood now. He was suspicious of her, of what she might know about him. "I..." What could she say?

"Don't dissemble now, Ms. Buchanan. If there is one thing I appreciate it's honesty. Especially from a woman."

What a strange sentiment to hear coming from the mouth of a man for whom subterfuge was undoubtedly a way of life!

Heather nodded. "All right. Let's just say that I've heard that you can be a bit intimidating."

He considered her with an unreadable gaze, revealing nothing of his thoughts, though for the first time she thought she might have detected a glint of humor in the depths of his eyes. "And *where* exactly did you hear that?"

"From one of my associates at the clinic. I received the impression that you made her extremely nervous when you were in last." That at least was the truth, although a bit of an understatement. Deb, the receptionist, had said that he'd almost had her in tears with his demands for intensive scheduling and intensive therapy that simply weren't possible with their current patient load. Now, Heather faced the same man and waited for him to pronounce her acceptable or unacceptable. And that frightened her to death.

She watched him walk haltingly across the room to the window then turn to study her. With the light at his back, his expression was in shadow.

The maneuver was no accident. Court had learned long ago to use even the smallest advantage, and he did so instinctively. He was a cautious man; a man who trusted nobody. Now, he weighed the response of the woman before him. She was good at thinking on her feet; there was no doubt about that.

"So then," he asked finally, "why are you here?" He suspected his chances of hearing the truth were not good. No matter how perfectly Ms. Buchanan might fit the role of his physical therapist, her sudden appearance when another man had been expected was suspicious. And, in his business, caution was a way of life. It kept him alive.

Heather drew a deep breath. "I need the work."

Simple response. Little chance of being caught in a lie there. "What are you going to do if I yell at you like I did your colleague?"

"Yell back," she said without hesitation. "I know my job, Mr. Gabriele, and I'm confident in my work."

His lips twitched, but he suppressed the urge to smile at her aura of supreme assurance. "Have you been with the Rockford Clinic long?" He was familiar with the clinic's personnel, and knew that, if indeed she was with them at all, she would have to be a new addition. Still, he was interested in hearing how she'd explain that.

"I just started with them actually, which is the

reason I was available to come here. I don't have my own client list yet.''

The last Court had heard, the clinic was fully staffed. He'd have to do some checking. Aloud, he said, ''I see.''

Were the truth to be told, he intensely disliked the idea of having an untrained female around in a situation that could turn dangerous at any moment. But, if she was his only option in getting his leg healed quickly, then he wasn't about to turn her away. At least not until he'd found a replacement for her.

''I was with the Northwest up until a few days ago,'' Heather continued. ''You can check my record if you like.''

''I'll do that.'' He studied her. Despite the loose fit of her jungle-print skirt and olive-green blouse, it was obvious to any man with eyes in his head that Heather Buchanan, if that was indeed her name, was an attractive woman. Some might even call her beautiful in a wholesome, natural way. Her russet-hued eyes sparkled in a way that made a man think of candlelight and wine. Her flame-tinged dark auburn hair flowed in tousled waves to the middle of her back in a manner that brought moonlight and rumpled sheets to mind. And her generous mouth with its pouty oh-so-kissable lips had a way of curving into the most innocent, and therefore sexiest, smile he'd seen in longer than he cared to admit. In fact, there was a virtuous aura about her that was enchanting. And that was a danger in itself. He didn't need the distraction.

Better the devil you know than the one you don't.

Court narrowed his eyes as the old adage echoed in his mind. It just might be good advice in this case.

As though a sudden thought had occurred to him, he looked at her sharply. ''Your employer did tell you that you'd be required to live in, didn't he? I want to be able to grab a few minutes of therapy between clients, whenever possible. Also, I'm an insomniac, Ms. Buchanan. And if I decide that an evening therapy session is what I need to help me sleep, I want my therapist available. The goal here is the speediest recovery possible. It is not an option. It is essential. I may want as many as four sessions in a day. Are we clear?''

''Of course.''

He nodded. ''All right, Ms. Buchanan, you can stay. For now. But you should know that I'll be putting in a request for a replacement. Someone more suitable to my situation.''

She nodded. ''Fine. I can accept that. At least I know where I stand.''

''I'll have Ernest show you to your room as soon as we're finished this morning.''

''Thank you.''

''You're welcome,'' he said. And then, for the first time since making her acquaintance, he smiled. It was a courteous smile, more a baring of teeth than a gesture of warmth, but it packed a wallop. Heather stared in amazement as the aura of darkness that mantled Court Gabriele momentarily lifted, transforming him into a truly handsome man. ''I'll go and put on that pair of exercise shorts you recommended,'' he said. ''And then, Ms. Buchanan, since we're obviously going to be working rather closely,

I think we should move to a first-name basis. Don't you?'' The question seemed rhetorical because he didn't give her time to respond before walking away.

Heather didn't know how long she stood staring after him, completely immobilized by the man's halfhearted smile. Good, Lord! If the simple flash of a set of strong white teeth affected her this way, how on earth was she going to be able to function when she had to touch that very attractive and virile body? Court Gabriele was a threat to her in ways she had never expected.

She closed her eyes and sighed. She had about five minutes to pull herself together. Five minutes to find her professional detachment and be prepared to do what was required of her.

She'd think of Des, that's what she'd do. She'd focus solely on her reason for being here, on the fact that Court Gabriele was in all likelihood a criminal of the worst sort. And she would most certainly not think about how long it had been since she had felt such interest in a man. Heaven only knew why, when she did finally feel the first faint stirring of attraction again, it had to be for a man like him. A man who lived in a world of violence. No matter which side of the law he was on, he was no different from Jay Caldwell in that respect. But she refused to think about Jay now. Her fiancé had been dead and gone for six years. There was nothing to be gained in living in the past.

With a muffled groan, she turned and focused on getting her equipment ready. And then she realized that her initial plan to check Gabriele's identification sometime during their workout had also been foiled.

Damn! He would undoubtedly leave his wallet in his room with his trousers.

Oh, well, at least she'd managed to get the job. But then failure hadn't been an option—not in her situation. Neither would it be an option in accomplishing the tasks that still faced her. Somehow she'd have to finagle other opportunities to check out Mr. Gabriele.

Purportedly, Gabriele was an influential Seattle lawyer. Unfortunately, his connection with Rick DiMona meant that he almost certainly operated on the fringes of legality. Either that, or—as DiMona himself had intimated at one point—it was possible that Gabriele was an undercover cop. But, whoever Court Gabriele was, the last thing Heather wanted him to discover was that she was working for DiMona. If he was of the same breed as DiMona, she'd probably wind up dead. If he was a cop, she'd be in jail for the rest of her life. Neither was an option she was willing to accept. Not with Des's life hanging in the balance.

Chapter 2

Court frowned as he made his way along the wide, red-tiled corridor of his southwestern-style residence and opened the door to the master suite. He didn't like the idea of having Heather Buchanan around. Or rather, considering the disturbing impulse he'd experienced to press his lips to that pounding pulse point in her throat, perhaps he liked the idea too much. He hadn't been distracted like that in a long time. He didn't need the distraction now. And he had little doubt that Heather Buchanan could prove to be one hell of a distraction.

But she wouldn't survive in his world. Not for long. An image of Heather strolling along a beach dressed in a tropical sari with a large white lotus blossom tucked behind her ear insinuated itself into his mind. That's the kind of woman she gave the impression of being. A bit exotic, naturally sensual.

The kind of woman who deserved to be made love to in the moonlight under a canopy of stars. Hell, she probably still believed in fairy-tale princes and magic kingdoms. And, unfortunately for her, he was not a white knight. Cynical DEA agents like Court Morgan, a.k.a. Court Gabriele, just weren't white knight material. Which meant that he needed to get her back out of his world as quickly as possible.

If he wasn't so desperate to get his leg working reliably again before everything went down, he'd be tempted to send her packing despite the probable expedience of keeping her where he could watch her. But current estimates suggested that he had six weeks, eight at the most, before he needed to be able to move around without the hindrance of an unreliable leg and a cane. With time constraints like that, he couldn't afford to send her away. Not until he had a replacement for her.

He had barely finished changing into a pair of black exercise shorts when the intercom buzzer sounded and the gritty voice belonging to his friend and DEA associate, Ernest Duke, demanded his attention. "Mr. Gabriele, Mr. Romano is here."

Court frowned. "We don't have an appointment, do we?"

"No, sir. But Mr. Romano says it will only take a few minutes."

He paused to think. "All right. Give me five minutes to get to my office. And you'd better inform Ms. Buchanan that our session will be postponed for about half an hour."

"Of course, sir."

Court grimaced. Judging by the number of sirs

suddenly peppering Ernest's speech, Romano must be within earshot of the exchange. "Oh, and Ernest. You might as well show her to her room while I'm meeting with Marc."

"Yes, sir."

Court looked down at himself and decided against changing back into his trousers. It might be a bit unprofessional to meet with Romano in exercise shorts and a T-shirt, but then Romano had arrived at his home without an appointment. Picking up his cane, Court made his way toward his office.

A moment after he got to his study, Ernest knocked and opened the double mahogany doors to show in a tall, dark man. "Hello, Marc," Court said as he moved forward to greet him, shaking his hand and clasping his elbow in the manner of a friendly business associate. The Colombian was dressed impeccably as always in a dove-grey business suit. He carried an expensive leather briefcase in his left hand. "How are you?"

"Fine. Fine. Hey, how's the leg? Not good, huh? You're not back to the office yet."

Court shrugged and moved toward his desk. "It's coming along. I was just about to have a therapy session." He indicated one of the two large leather chairs in front of his desk. "Have a seat."

Romano set the briefcase down beside the chair, opened the bottom button on his suit jacket and sat.

"So, how's it going?" Court asked, seating himself at his desk. "How's the wife? And, Mercedes, is she doing well in school?" He uttered the questions automatically, playing the courteous associate even as he studied Romano, seeking nuances in tone or expression that might explain the unexpected visit.

Marc nodded. "Everyone's fine. Mercedes—" he waved his hands and shrugged "—she is a teenager. What is there to say?"

"I understand." Flipping open the box of Cuban cigars on his desk—a gift from the Colombians— Court raised an eyebrow in question as he proffered the box to Romano.

Romano waved it away with his thanks and tapped the briefcase at his side meaningfully. "I haven't much time today, and I have some business to discuss with you."

"Of course." Without any further discourse, Court turned on the stereo. Music flowed from six speakers spaced throughout the room. The interference the music provided to any directional mikes would be minimal at best given the recent advances in listening devices, but the gesture seemed to provide at least some assurance to his nervous clients. And Gabriele had worked hard to earn a reputation as a cautious man. He'd had to earn the trust of his associates. And that meant he had to keep their interests uppermost in his mind at all times.

Now, Court nodded at Romano to continue.

Marc Romano placed the briefcase on his lap, backward, and flipped it open briefly to reveal the contents. Court saw rows upon rows of greenbacks. Five-hundred thousand dollars easily. Illicit profits. Drug money. Money that Court Gabriele's client needed to have laundered.

Court lifted his eyes to Romano's face. In any other place and time, if he had been unaware of Ro-

mano's business, he would actually have liked the
man. But here and now he could not forget that it
was men like Romano who put poison onto the
streets. Poison that killed kids and wrecked lives.
Poison whose only purpose was to allow Romano
and others like him to profit from human suffering.
It was a man like Romano who had been responsible
for the death of Court's sister, Carly. And, it was
Romano's associates who had killed his best friend
and partner, Brett Sanders.

They'd used a woman to get to Brett, Court re-
called. The memory had him vowing silently to be
doubly wary of Ms. Buchanan until he knew for certain she was legitimate.

Now, he met the dark-eyed gaze of the man seated
across from him. There was nothing he wanted more
than to see the Colombians pay for their crimes.
When the shipment that everyone was awaiting finally arrived and the time came to move in, they
would pay. They would all pay dearly. He'd promised himself that. Yet, for the moment, Court was
forced to bury those feelings and focus on the exe-
cution of his job. "When do you need it?"

"A couple of months. No longer."

"I'll let you know where I set up the accounts."

"Fine," Romano responded with another nod.
Snapping the briefcase closed, he set it on the floor
near his chair. "There is something else."

Court waved a hand in invitation, but said nothing.

"I have a friend who would like to meet with you.
Perhaps to do business. You interested?"

"A friend?" Court quizzed.

Romano hedged. "An acquaintance."

"Does this acquaintance have a name?"

"Kostenka. Alek Kostenka."

Court concealed his surprise. He'd heard that the cartel was getting into bed with other crime organizations, but he hadn't expected to encounter a connection himself. Interesting. Court needed to buy himself some time. "I'll talk to him, but not until I'm back at the office." His tone made it clear that, at this point, he was promising nothing more than a meeting. He'd pass Kostenka's name on and see how exactly they wanted him to handle the situation.

"Good enough."

Romano stood while Court notified Ernest that their guest was leaving. Then, grasping his cane, Court retrieved the briefcase, which he placed in the safe concealed behind the wood-paneled wall and turned to show Romano out. Before he had quite caught up with him, Marc opened the study door and stopped short. "Well, well. You've been holding out on me, Court," he said. "*Who* is this?"

Court was reasonably certain of the identity of the person who'd prompted the rather enthusiastic question from his client. Nevertheless, he stepped around the edge of the door to check.

He was right.

Heather Buchanan stood in the corridor looking ill at ease and much too attractive for her own good. Damn it! Why couldn't she have stayed out of sight? If she was legitimate, the last thing he wanted was to bring her to the attention of people like Romano. Adjusting his tone to impart a distance he didn't feel, he said, "Marc Romano this is Heather Buchanan.

Ms. Buchanan, Marc Romano.'' He met Romano's questioning gaze. "Ms. Buchanan is my physical therapist…for the present.''

"Ah.''

Court waited while Marc extended a hand to Heather and they exchanged pleasantries. Then he asked, "Can I help you, Heather?''

"Oh, no, I'm fine. I just went out to my car for a second. I'd forgotten one of my cases.'' She lifted her hand to reveal a small black hard-sided case. Then, looking at Marc, she said, "It was nice meeting you, Mr. Romano.'' Court thought her smile seemed a bit strained. Tense? Afraid? Why?

Marc smiled. "The pleasure was mine, Ms. Buchanan, I assure you.'' Then, before she could respond, he turned to Court. "No need for you to see me out with that leg of yours the way it is, Court,'' he said. "I'm sure I can find the way.''

Court nodded and offered his hand in farewell. "A pleasure doing business with you, Marc, as always. Ernest will get the door.''

He watched his client head down the hall, and then turned back to Ms. Buchanan. "Well, Heather, since we're going in the same direction, allow me to carry the case for you.''

"Oh, no, that's all right. I'm used to it.''

"I insist.'' Taking the case from her fingers, he turned and began to walk in the direction of the gym leaving her no choice but to fall into step with him. With a slight frown on her forehead, she walked along at his side, staring at the floor. He wondered what she was thinking. Then, as the weight of the case tugged at his arm, he frowned. "What exactly are you carrying in here, Heather? Bricks?"

"Naw, just my Uzi and my combat boots," she muttered. The response was glib, automatic.

That was original! Surprised, Court almost grinned. "Pardon me?" he couldn't help asking.

She started visibly at his question. Her head snapped up, her eyes widened and her freckles suddenly stood out with interesting clarity against the paleness of her complexion. Had his tone been that sharp? he wondered. Or did Ms. Buchanan have something to be worried about?

"Just kidding!" She offered him a smile that looked a bit forced and laughed. "I'm asked that question so often—about my purse and my cases—that I've made a habit of just offering the same flippant response every time."

Court nodded, but wondered at the flash of apprehension he'd discerned in her eyes. "No need to apologize. I know a joke when I hear one." What reason had Ms. Buchanan to fear that her offhand response would be taken for anything other than a wisecrack? What did she know, or think she knew?

He didn't like the implications involved here. And considering his own situation, he'd better get Edison checking her out as soon as possible.

They entered the gym and he set the case down for her. "I'll just be a moment, Heather. I need to make a quick call."

"All right."

A call to one of the local flower shops would be heard by his people—who kept a tap on his line for just that purpose—and they would set up a meeting with Edison. That would start the wheels turning in discovering the answers to the questions that had been bothering him the most since the moment he'd laid eyes on his new physical therapist. Who exactly *was* Heather Buchanan? What the devil was she doing here so suddenly? And did she have something to be afraid of?

He checked his watch and decided to order the flowers to be delivered tomorrow, which would translate to a meeting at 5:00 p.m. today.

One way or another, he was going to find out everything there was to know about Ms. Buchanan because instinct told him that her presence here was no accident. He considered that pounding pulse point in her throat again. Hell, the research could prove interesting as long as he kept his focus where it needed to be.

Then he frowned furiously. Damn! He was already thinking up excuses *not* to maintain his distance from the lovely therapist. So much for willpower. He really was going to have to find out what had happened to Miguel. Soon.

By the time Gabriele returned to the gym, Heather had managed to gather the tatters of her professional reserve into place. "I'd like to test your sensory level first," she said, her words clipped and all business. Studiously avoiding his unsettling gaze, she focused on the work at hand. "I'm going to touch your leg lightly with a needle in several spots, and I want you to tell me whether I'm using the dull or sharp end of the needle. Then we'll do a test for temperature sensitivity, and I'll get you to distinguish between hot and cold. All right?''

''Sure.'' She could feel his gaze on her face. Probing. Astute. As tangible as a touch. And much too intelligent. How long could she hope to fool him?

No! She wouldn't think about that. She needed to concentrate on learning what DiMona wanted to know and then get out of both Gabriele's and DiMona's lives. DiMona wanted to know everything about Court Gabriele from the details of his medical condition—a violation of patient confidentiality, but she really didn't have much choice—to whom Court met and when. Fine, she could handle that. Then, with any luck she'd leave here and never see either one of them again.

''Why don't you sit on the table?'' She indicated the massage table in one corner of his private gym. She wondered if it, like much of his extensive exercise equipment, had been in place all along, or whether he'd had it specifically installed at the clinic's behest as he had the parallel bars.

He moved toward the table without comment.

He had good legs, she noted, long and straight. Solid thighs. Nice knees, not knobby. Well-defined calves. They were even nicely tanned beneath the fine dusting of dark hair.

Ever mindful of DiMona's desire to know everything, she allowed her curiosity free reign. ''You have a nice tan, Mr. Gabriele. Are you an outdoor sports enthusiast?''

He shrugged. ''I suppose you could say that,'' he responded as he got settled on the table. ''Swimming, hiking, golf, the occasional tennis match.''

She pulled a chair up before him where she could sit comfortably to examine him. So far, so good. Now, if she could only forget the presence of the man and focus exclusively on his injured leg, she'd be fine. But, of course, she couldn't do that.

"What about you?"

His voice startled her. "I'm sorry. What about me?"

"Do you like outdoor sports?"

She nodded. "I like hiking. I used to like fishing with my father when I was little."

Okay, first she had to verify that his damaged leg was still cold to the touch in comparison with his healthy one. Reaching out, she gently laid her hands over his knees.

Her palms tingled as an intense current of sexual awareness passed between them. She was suddenly acutely aware of the texture of the fine dark hairs on his legs, of the faint scent of his aftershave, of…him. Everything about him. Focusing with difficulty on the medical examination she was supposed to be conducting, she gritted her teeth and moved her hands slightly, seeking the spot on his thigh where the temperature differential faded. There. But moving her hands had only intensified the sensation in her palms. Embarrassingly, she felt herself begin to flush. Not for the first time in her life she cursed her fair complexion. Damn it anyway. She was being sabotaged by hormones and pheromones.

She removed her hands rather hastily, managing to stop just short of jerking them back.

"Is something wrong, Heather?"

Heather swallowed and grimaced inwardly. She

should have known he was much too perceptive not to notice. "I—I" she stammered, seeking a believable response. "It's just a little warm in here."

"Is it?" Was it just her, or did his voice hold a quality of intimacy that should not have been there?

She felt her flush intensify and kept her head down. "I think so. Yes." Heavens above! What was the matter with her? Court Gabriele should have been just another patient. She should have been able to maintain her professional distance despite the situation. But he wasn't, and apparently she couldn't.

Perhaps her own fear of the situation was heightening her perceptions. That was probably it. And somehow, she'd just have to find a way to work around that.

"I hadn't noticed." His tone was definitely suggestive. "So, what do you think?"

"What do I think?" she echoed in confusion.

"My leg," he clarified.

Heather swallowed and concentrated on her work. "As you said, there is still an obvious difference in temperature. Your left knee is warmer. I'll know more once we've finished here." She reached for her case of supplies. "Look straight ahead, not at what I'm doing. All right?"

"Sure."

She gently touched his thigh with the sharp end of the needle. "Tell me what you feel. Sharp or dull?"

"Sharp," he replied without hesitation as he rubbed briefly at the spot. She moved the needle nearer the knee area and he frowned, concentrating longer on his response this time. "Dull, I think."

They continued the process for a few minutes, covering the thigh, knee and calf area. After a few minutes of testing, she made some notes on his chart.

"Well," he prompted. "What's the verdict?" Any suggestion of intimacy that may have been in his tone earlier was gone. He sounded authoritative and impatient.

"You have sensation, but it's not distinct." She glanced at him but quickly lowered her eyes before she could be unsettled by his piercing look. "You can tell when you're being touched, but you often have trouble differentiating between a sharp and a dull feeling—particularly in the knee area. Let's try hot and cold."

She put the needle carefully back into its case and withdrew the warm-and-cold Gel Packs. She laid the warm one over his knee. "Warm or cold?"

He frowned, concentrating. "I can tell it's there because I can sense the pressure, but that's all. I can't feel it."

Heather nodded and switched Gel Packs. "This one?"

After a moment, his expression cleared. "Definitely cold." She removed the pack and made a note. "Uncomfortably cold," he added, reaching to rub his knee again.

"What do you mean?"

"Even after you took it off, it was as though the cold just kept going deeper and deeper. The same thing happened when I picked up a cat and it dug its claws in. Even after I put it down, I couldn't get rid of the feeling of claws digging in."

Heather nodded. "That's a pain echo. It happens

sometimes when the nerves seem to short-circuit, broadcasting the same message over and over again. Which means that some of the surface nerves are still working, and they're probably trying to compensate for the ones that aren't.'' She paused, rubbing his knee hard to warm it. ''Is that better?''

He nodded. ''Much.''

Removing her hand, she considered his wounded leg thoughtfully. ''I'm not surprised that cold bothers you. Damaged nerves do tend to be sensitive to cold. I'm a bit concerned, though, that you couldn't sense the warmer pack. You'll have to be careful. You could burn yourself quite badly without realizing it.''

''I'll be careful.'' His tone was definitely impatient now. ''It's the strength I'm concerned about. I need a leg that won't collapse on me without warning.''

Heather nodded. ''All right, Mr. Gabriele, we'll focus on that for the first while. We'll try the stationary bike first, shall we? To see how much range of motion you have?''

''Court.''

Heather looked up in confusion, confounded by the single word coming out of nowhere. ''What?''

''Call me, Court. Remember?''

Heather considered. She really didn't want to become any more familiar with him than she already was, but she'd already seen enough of Court Gabriele to know that he was a very obstinate man. She'd be better served saving her energy for more important battles. ''All right, Court.'' Then, with a

gesture of her arm she indicated that he should proceed to the stationery bike.

"Do you have dinner plans, Heather?"

She whirled to look at him, stunned by the question, hoping to perceive some indication of his mo-
tivation from his countenance. "Not really. Why?"

Leaning on his cane, he met her gaze with an
impenetrable look of his own. "We have dinner at
seven. Or did Ernest tell you?"

Oh, that's all it was. She felt foolish now for having read anything more into a such a simple question. "No," she murmured. "No, he didn't."

Gabriele nodded, studying her for a moment as
though seeking something in her face. "I have a
formal dining room, but I seldom use it. Too preten-
tious for small gatherings. I hope you won't be dis-
appointed if I ask you to join me in the breakfast
nook for dinner tonight."

"Of course not. I'll look forward to it."

"Will you?" He eyed her with a curiously intent
expression, and Heather received the distinct impression that there were nuances to this conversation
that she'd missed entirely.

Chapter 3

Oh, Des, what did you get us into? Heather asked silently as she stood in the room to which she'd been shown, staring out at the luxurious textures of Court Gabriele's professionally landscaped yard. Flowers in vibrant hues of color set against a palate of varying shades of green drew the eye like a magnet, but the picture in her mind's eye was a totally different one.

She remembered the choking fear of receiving a call from the hospital advising her that her brother had been admitted. She remembered rushing down there, only to find out that his injuries—rather than being the result of an accident—had been deliberately inflicted. As a warning. She remembered Des struggling to tell her what had happened while still attempting to protect her from the truth. But there was no protection, no reassurance to be had.

With his handsome face distorted by bruises, one of his eyes swollen shut, and his thick black hair half concealed by white bandages, Des barely resembled the younger brother she'd raised for the last ten years. "Who did this?" Heather had demanded of him as soon as he was able to talk.

He'd tried to wave away her question, grimacing at the pain of the movement. "Nobody you know, Sis. Some people…people that I owe money to."

For an instant she could only stare at him, trying to understand. But, try as she might, understanding refused to come. "Money! How could you owe money to people who would do this to you?"

Des had closed his eyes tightly. "God, why can't I ever do anything right? I only wanted to help. To earn some money so that you wouldn't have to work so hard." He'd opened his eyes then, fixing his gaze on her with a new light of determination in his eyes. "Look, just don't worry about it, okay? I'll take care of it."

But Heather wasn't prepared to let it go that easily. "Desmond Buchanan, you will tell me what is going on, and you will tell me this instant. Do you understand? Because I'm going to find out. One way or another."

Avoiding her gaze, he stared out the window next to his bed. Finally, he shrugged. "Okay. But you aren't going to like it."

Heather frowned. "I don't like it *now*."

He stared at the bedcovers, avoiding her eyes, and began. "You know that I wasn't getting very good grades." Heather made an affirmative noise, and he continued. "Well, with you working so hard to put me through college, I couldn't afford to flunk out. So, I started taking meth...you know, just to get through exams and stuff.'' He looked toward Heather then, as though to gauge her reaction. But she was too stunned to react. Her baby brother, the child she'd all but raised, was taking drugs! ''I didn't think I'd get hooked on them, Heather. Please believe that.''

Heather could only look at him in stunned amazement. How could her brother have become an addict without her realizing it? Of course they'd scarcely seen each other except in passing the last few months. She'd been busy working as many hours as she could in an attempt to drag them out of the financial hole they'd gotten themselves into. Or rather that *she* had gotten them into by relying on credit cards to take up the slack in their finances. And she'd been making headway. But at what cost?

When Heather didn't respond, Des continued. ''Well anyway...the meth was expensive, you know, and I couldn't afford it on the kind of money I was making at the tire shop. A friend suggested that I might want to go into business for myself. You know, sell the stuff on campus.''

This time Heather couldn't control her reaction. ''You started dealing drugs!''

''Not much. Just enough to earn some extra money.'' Des's expression was guilt-stricken and remorseful, but neither guilt nor remorse could reverse the deed.

Heather could only shake her head. ''My God! What were you thinking?''

He flashed her a resentful look. ''I was thinking

that I couldn't let you down again. I'm tired of failing at everything I do.''

It was a familiar litany and Heather couldn't allow
herself to be drawn down the same old self-pitying
path. ''All right! All right! Just forget that for the
moment. Just who is it that you owe money to? And,
how much?''

Des stared sullenly down at the blanket. ''I owe
it to a guy named Herrera. He's my supplier.''

''How much?''

Des swallowed, then looked at Heather with tears
in his one good eye. ''Ten thousand,'' he murmured.

Stunned, Heather sank wordlessly down onto the
chair next to the bed. Ten thousand! It might as well
have been ten million. There was no way she could
come up with that kind of money. Her credit was
stretched to the limit, and she knew her bank would
not extend credit without adequate security. Security
which she didn't have.

''I wish they'd just killed me last night, and got
it over with,'' Des said bitterly.

''Don't say that!'' Heather ordered sharply. Her
mind raced as she tried to find a way out of the
predicament. ''How long did they give you to get
the money?'' she asked.

''A week.''

Not long enough. She shook her head in despair.
''What did you do with the money, Des? Maybe we
can sell what you bought with it, or…''

''I didn't buy anything, Sis.'' Avoiding her gaze
once more, he stared out the window. ''I bet it on a
horse race. The race was supposed to be fixed.

That's what they told me. I figured I'd at least double my money. But…''

''You lost it,'' Heather concluded for him.

He nodded miserably and she saw the tortured, lonely child beneath the facade of the bruised nineteen-year-old young man. Once, long ago, she'd failed him. He'd called her for help, and she'd muddled everything. She'd spent her life trying to make it up to him. To be mother and father and sister. But somehow, she'd never seemed quite equal to the task.

Now, if she didn't help him get out of this, she stood to lose the only family member she had left, the only person in the world she loved. Leaning forward, she lay her hand over his. ''We'll get through this, Des. Somehow. I'll think of something. In the meantime, I'll speak with the doctor about getting you some help.''

That had been three weeks ago. Des was healing now, and the rehab center was helping him kick his drug habit. Heather just hoped that the cost, to both of them, would not be more than they could live with.

Her watch alarm beeped, jerking her back to the present with a jolt. It was almost time to call in and retrieve her voice-mail messages. Time to pick up any further instructions DiMona might have left for her. Time to pay for her brother's life. And, since she'd been told not to risk calling from here unless she could be certain that no one could listen in on the call, that meant finding the nearest pay phone.

She found a convenience store about a mile down the road from Court's place that had a pay phone.

She'd just completed her call and discovered with a sense of relief that DiMona had left her no further instructions, when she heard the scrape of a shoe on pavement.

"Something wrong with the phone in your room, Heather?"

She whirled. Court! "Oh," she gasped, placing a hand over her pounding heart. "You startled me." What was he doing here?

One of his thick, black brows inched up, but his predatory golden eyes never wavered. "Really? I'd never have guessed." His gaze flicked to the pay phone and back. "I asked you if something was wrong with the phone at the house."

"No. No, of course not," Heather replied as her mind raced for a plausible explanation. "I was just planning on shopping for a few things and remembered that I'd forgotten to let one of my friends know that I wouldn't be home for a while. I thought I'd better call while I was thinking of it. I wouldn't want to forget again. She's the type who might call out the National Guard if she thought I'd gone missing."

He studied her for what seemed like an aeon although it was probably no more than a minute. And, as he looked deep into her eyes, Heather had the impression that he was trying to see straight through to her soul. Her heart began to pound as she ruthlessly resisted the almost overpowering urge to look away from his gaze. If only he wasn't so... magnetic...so dangerous. If only she didn't have to fear him.

Finally, in a neutral tone, he said, "Friends like that are hard to come by."

"Yes," Heather agreed a little too breathlessly. She cleared her throat. "Yes, they are." When he still didn't move away, she began to sidle past him. "Well, I'd better get my shopping done."

He nodded and turned slightly, allowing her to pass. But when Heather looked out the window of the store a moment later, she noted that he was still there. Watching her. *He suspects something,* her mind screamed. Taking a deep breath, hoping against hope that he would leave and go about his business, she ignored him and began shopping for articles she didn't need. Hardly even conscious of her choices, she resisted the urge to look toward him again…for a while. Finally, she could stand the suspense no longer.

She heaved a sigh of relief. He was gone!

At five o'clock, Ernest drove Court into the parking garage of a downtown shopping complex. After taking a quick but thorough look around, Court made his way toward the elevator while Ernest stayed with the car. Within seconds, another man exited a vehicle some distance away and began converging on the lift as well.

Court gave him a casual glance.

Entering the elevator, Court pressed the button for the main level, then politely held the door for the other man to enter. He was a blond man of average height and looks with kind but astute green eyes. He nodded his thanks and pressed the button for the upper level.

The elevator door closed. "Edison," Court greeted him. "I need some information."

"Good to see you too, Court. Always wonderful talking to you."

"Yeah, you, too. Now let's get to the point."

"Sure. What do you need to know?"

"Everything there is to know about Heather Buchanan, a resident of Seattle. Physical therapist. Says she just started working for the Rockford Clinic, but worked at the Northwest Hospital before that. And, I need it yesterday."

Edison shrugged. "You got it. May I ask why?"

"That guy, Miguel, that was supposed to show up at my place, never showed. She's there in his place, and my gut tells me there's something not quite right about her."

Edison frowned. "Okay, I'm on it. I'll have preliminary info for you tonight if you can get away."

Court nodded. "Ten-thirty at Mario's." Mario's was a small, but exclusive club that he frequented. "I've got a name for you, too. A Russian connection. Wants to meet with me."

Edison's expression didn't alter. He'd be deadly at poker. "What's the name?" he asked.

"Alek Kostenka."

He nodded. "I'll pass it on."

"Any news for me?" Court asked.

Edison shook his head. "Nothing's changed so far. Channing misses his house."

Court smiled with grim satisfaction. "I don't blame him. It's a nice place. Tell him I'm enjoying it."

Parker Channing was the crooked lawyer whose

home and practice Court had taken over. Since the lawyer's home would have been surrendered under the laws of forfeiture anyway, the DEA had managed to convince him to cooperate in exchange for a second chance with a new identity. The Colombians had, of course, been suspicious of Channing's death and Gabriele's sudden appearance. But, careful planning had ensured that there'd been nothing for them to find to confirm their suspicions. Then, Court had simply waited for them to approach him with the same kind of deal they'd offered Channing. It had taken time, but finally the plan had begun to work.

Edison nodded. "I'll do that. I'm sure it will ease his mind."

"Right," Court drawled as the elevator stopped. He exited, going directly to a men's wear store where he browsed for a minute, purchased a tie and then left. His thoughts returned to Heather Buchanan. He hated waiting to find out what it was about her that had his instincts clamoring, but there wasn't much he could do about it.

None of the family pictures on the wall in the living room had Court in them. How odd!

Heather began another thorough perusal of the wall of photographs she'd discovered, just to be sure. No mistake. Although there were a few pictures of children, none of them bore the slightest resemblance to her host. The pictures were primarily of an older couple that Heather assumed to be Court's parents taken in varying locations from cityscapes to country with one tropical setting. Perhaps Hawaii.

Some of the photos included other people. Aunts and uncles, perhaps. One included a much older couple. Grandparents? But nowhere was there a picture of Court.

"Are you a photography buff?"

Court's voice startled her and she whirled to see him lounging in the doorway. His relaxed stance suggested he'd been observing her for some time.

"No. No, but I'm a bit of a genealogist, and I like to see a moment in someone's family history captured forever in a picture. Are these your parents?"

"Mm-hm."

"Are you in any of these pictures?" she asked, trying to be tactful although she was virtually positive of the answer.

He shook his head. "Those were all taken before I was born. The ones that include me are over here." He indicated a small alcove that Heather hadn't noticed.

"Oh. Do you mind if I look?"

"Of course not."

Heather stepped into the alcove. It was more of a narrow hallway actually with a glass wall overlooking the solarium and the pool. The alcove contained an antique Spanish-looking chest draped with an equally aged throw rug, a number of potted plants, and a wall of photographs. Yes, Court was definitely in some of these. She sighed inwardly. One more thing on DiMona's list that she could confirm.

Lord, she hated this…this subterfuge.

Suddenly, as she moved along the wall scanning the pictures, one of them seemed to reach out to halt her. It was a school picture of Court. He looked happy and mischievous. The shadows that lurked in his eyes now hadn't existed yet. Then, his golden eyes had danced with the playful light of youth.

She looked at him where he leaned silently against the doorway, simply watching her. "How old were you here?"

He glanced at thc photo. "Seven, I think. Why?"

She shrugged. "You look like you were a little devil."

He raised a brow. "A bit of a prankster perhaps."

Heather smiled and concluded, "A handful."

The corners of his mouth curved slightly. "Maybe," he allowed. Then, checking his watch, he added. "Well, I guess it's time I got ready for dinner. I'll leave you to your pictorial history studies."

Heather watched him go. She sensed that there were more layers to Court Gabriele than an onion. Was that what DiMona perceived? she wondered. And now, it was her job to peel away the layers until she discovered the core of the man within. Closing her eyes, she took a deep breath. She wasn't sure she was up to the task.

Court arrived in the kitchen for dinner to find Heather already present and chatting comfortably with his housekeeper, Elizabeth Kaiser. Liz Kaiser was a slightly overweight, motherly-looking woman in her mid to late forties whom no one would suspect of having DEA affiliations. In addition, her situation as a widow with grown children, made her an ideal candidate for her current post. There was nobody to complain if she was away from home for a while.

Heather, apparently having offered to help, placed

a plate of fresh rolls on the table and then turned to study the circular nook area with its huge bank of windows. "The view from here must be absolutely incredible in the daylight," she commented.

"Yes, it is," Liz responded. "The house is high enough to have a nice view of the ocean as well as a portion of the city. There's nothing quite so beautiful as the view of Seattle at night from the pool area, though."

Heather turned toward her right, taking in the partial view of a million sparkling city lights. "It is beautiful but...I don't know. Somehow, cityscapes at night always make me feel lonely."

"Do you live alone?" Court asked from the doorway.

Heather jumped slightly at the sound of his voice. "Yes," she said, turning to face him. "Yes, I live alone."

The slight hesitation, the tone of her voice, made him suspect that she was being less than truthful. Interesting. He wondered whom she lived with. A boyfriend? A roommate? And why would she feel it necessary to lie?

Liz looked at Court and smiled. "Good evening, Court. Dinner will be on shortly if you want to have a seat. I've left the wine to breathe." She indicated a bottle of white wine chilling in an ice bucket on the table.

"Thank you, Liz. What's on the menu?"

"Salmon steak and Caesar salad."

"Sounds great," Court murmured, but the comment was automatic for, in truth, he'd barely absorbed Liz's response before his attention had returned to Heather.

Wearing a cream-colored outfit in some layered, gauzy fabric, she stood in profile, silhouetted against the night-blackened windows of the breakfast nook. She looked pensive and…somehow vulnerable. Court felt a stirring of masculine protectiveness that he had not expected to feel. Shaking his head slightly as though to displace the image and the emotion, he looked away and crossed the room to the table. The last thing he needed was to be sucker punched by sentiment.

As he hooked his cane over the back of his chair, the slight clatter disturbed Heather and she turned toward him. For an instant, just an instant, naked, unguarded emotion shone from her eyes, intense but impossible to interpret. And then it was gone, cloaked by a forced smile.

Keeping the knee of his injured leg carefully locked so that it wouldn't fail on him, Court walked around the table without his cane to pull out her chair. "Have a seat, Heather," he invited.

"Thank you," she murmured as she complied.

She sat there with her hands folded in her lap wondering what she could possibly accomplish when she couldn't even look at Court Gabriele without her stomach fluttering like a schoolgirl's. Which, when she thought about it, didn't make the slightest bit of sense. She'd seen men who were more handsome—she'd even worked with some of them—and none of them had affected her in the least. So why did Court Gabriele wreak such havoc on her senses?

Forcing herself to focus on her reason for being

there, Heather took a slow deep breath and attempted
to invoke a calmness she didn't feel. She needed to
draw him out and find out all there was to know
about him. She needed to be sophisticated and in-
quisitive while giving the impression of being only
casually interested in his responses. But most of all,
she needed to be immune to whatever it was about
him that sent her senses into chaos.

"Is something wrong, Heather?" he asked.

Her gaze flew up to meet his and she found herself
pinned by his too perceptive predator's eyes.
"Wrong? No, of course not. Why do you ask?"

He shrugged. "You seem a bit pensive. Wine?"
he asked, changing tack so quickly she was left
floundering.

"Oh…um, yes. Thank you." She waited while he
poured, using the time to marshal her resources.
"So, how long have you lived in Seattle?"

"Not long actually, although I guess it's going on
two years now. Just since my friend, Parker Channing, passed away. He wanted me to take over his
legal practice, and he left the house to me."

"Oh, I'm sorry." Heather frowned thoughtfully,
sipping her wine, and then asked, "Isn't it unusual
for a lawyer to leave his practice to someone who's
not a partner?"

"We were partners out East at one time. And,
he'd been in the process of talking me into moving
out here and joining his firm when he was killed."

"I see." Heather sipped her wine again. "Did you
say he was killed?"

"Yes. In a boating accident."

"Oh." At least he wasn't shot, she mused—which

was what she more than half feared she might hear. "I'm sorry," she said again.

"Yeah." Court cleared his throat. "Me, too." And so the evening went. After Liz Kaiser had served their dinner and retired to her room, Heather learned little more to complete her picture of just who Court Gabriele was. A few tidbits, none of which seemed significant. She'd learned that Court had inherited Channing's junior partner—a young man named Doug Grey—and that Mr. Grey was handling the day-to-day operations of the law firm downtown while Court recuperated. She'd learned that Court had been working for a large law firm in New York prior to coming here, but was not a partner. And, she'd learned that Court was an outdoor sports enthusiast but that he'd never really enjoyed team sports, other than football. Not much information. Certainly not enough to satisfy DiMona.

She was racking her brain to try to figure out another course to take when Court spoke. "That therapeutic massage you mentioned earlier...will it help with insomnia?"

Heather set down her glass, studying his face carefully. "Has your leg been bothering you at night?"

He shook his head. "No. It did initially. I had to sleep with it propped on a pillow. But now I think it's just that I have a lot on my mind. Tension."

She nodded. "If tension is the problem, then a massage should definitely be helpful." For him anyway. She couldn't say what giving him a massage was going to do for her own attempts to sleep.

She lingered over her meal and then insisted on loading the dishwasher, but finally Court's promised therapeutic massage could be put off no longer. Perhaps she'd find the means to check his identification during the massage.

If there was anything more compelling than Court Gabriele in suit pants and a T-shirt, it was Court Gabriele nearly nude. Heather stared at the man lying on his stomach on the table before her wearing only a small white towel draped over his narrow hips, and, beneath that, a pair of briefs. Her mouth went dry and she swallowed reflexively, trying to dredge up some moisture.

Physically, he was gorgeous. There was simply no other word for it. He'd kept himself in superb condition with weight-lifting and exercise. His shoulders were wide, his torso tanned and muscular, his waist narrow. *He's a criminal, Heather. Remember that,* she told herself.

He could be a cop, another part of her brain argued.

Turning away from him, she concentrated on completing the preparation of the oils she planned to use. *Cops are no better,* she continued the internal argument with herself. *They get themselves killed.* There was no argument for that, and she was able to turn back to the man on the table with her professional reserve once more firmly in place.

But in winning the argument, she'd removed the barricade from memories that now refused to be caged. Memories of Jay. The man who'd taken both her and Des under his wing ten years ago when they'd had no one else in the world to help them. The man who'd taught her how to achieve her independence. The man who'd given her love and made her fall in love with him only to get himself killed three weeks before they were to have been married. Lord, she still missed him.

"What's that smell?" Court's voice startled her from her thoughts.

"Smell?" Heather cleared her throat, buying time to organize her thoughts. "Let's see. I've used sandalwood, cypress and a touch of apricot kernel in a base of sweet almond oil."

"It's nice."

"Yes. Let me just get a bit of cinnamon oil to set out, and we'll begin."

"Sure." His response was lazy. Almost sleepy. Taking a deep breath, she girded herself to do what she had to do.

Keeping her gaze on him, she moved across the room to check the pockets of the casual khaki trousers he'd removed. Empty. Damn. He must have left his ID in his room. Okay, so she'd simply have to get into his room. Soon!

Chapter 4

"Ready?" Heather asked as the essence of cinnamon began to compliment the other scents in the room.

"Mm-hm," Court responded. He'd been lying there trying to think of a way to draw Heather out, but, thus far, inspiration had deserted him so he decided to simply enjoy the massage while he worked on the problem.

Time lagged. As Heather's magic hands eased tension from his neck, shoulders and back, he found himself relaxing beneath her adept ministrations to the point that he almost fell asleep. Damn! It felt good. *Real* good. Too good. But he had a job to do. The last thing he needed was to allow Ms. Buchanan to lull him into complacency.

She began to massage the soles of his feet, and

he barely stifled a groan of ecstasy. A man could get used to having hands like that at his disposal.

The thought, when it occurred, was completely innocent, but in an instant some wicked part of himself turned it over and began to weave an intriguing fantasy around it. His body responded, forcing him to shift slightly into a more comfortable position, and he made a noise of self-disgust. Thank God, he was lying on his stomach.

"Did I hurt you?" Heather's throaty voice, soft and innocent, drew him back to the here and now.

"No. Are we about done?" His tone was more abrupt than he'd intended.

Her hands stilled. "I thought you wanted a massage."

"I did, but I have some things to do."

"Well, I'm sorry, but you can't rush a massage and still do it properly. Next time, you'll have to ensure that you've set aside enough time."

"Right. So, how much longer?"

"We're almost finished. Five, maybe ten minutes."

Five or ten minutes of pure sensual torture…or bliss depending on your point of view. Court nodded and focused his attention where it ought to be: on business.

Before dinner, he'd taken a couple of minutes to call the clinic and ask the administrator just what had happened to the man that they'd said they would send. He was told that Miguel had taken an extended vacation. A scheduled vacation? No, it was rather sudden. They'd assumed that perhaps he'd had a family emergency. Court had then placed an order for a male therapist to replace Ms. Buchanan as soon as possible. Is there a problem with her, sir? No, he just didn't want a woman around, especially a young one. It tended to provoke problems in his relationships. That was a lie, since he didn't have a relationship at present, but he couldn't very well tell the administrator that he didn't like the idea of putting an untrained female in possible peril, no matter how remote the possibility might be. The administrator said that, of course, he understood, and they'd terminated the conversation.

Court didn't like the sound of the suddenness of Miguel's departure. Miguel had taken an unscheduled vacation and Heather Buchanan had taken over his job—which planted her firmly in his household. It sounded a bit too coincidental, didn't it?

He needed to find out everything he could about Ms. Heather Buchanan—no matter how innocent she appeared. "Do you have a family, Heather?"

Her hands stilled on his body, then, "No. I'm not married."

"Parents?"

"My parents both died when I was a teenager."

"I'm sorry," he said. And he was. He didn't like the thought of somebody who exuded innocence and vulnerability the way Heather Buchanan did, being alone in the chaotic and troublesome teenage years. "Any brothers or sisters?"

Again her hands went still. A pause, then, "No."

She wasn't being exactly loquacious, which suggested discomfort with the topic. He decided to try a different one. "So, do you enjoy working in physical therapy?"

"Yes, of course. It's all I ever wanted to do."

"Ever?" he echoed.

"Mm-hm. Ever since I witnessed the misery my grandmother went through trying to claw her way back to a functioning existence after having a stroke. I knew then that I wanted to be able to help people."

Her response was more open. The truth, Court decided. "How old were you then?"

"Hm," her hands slowed as she thought. "I guess I would have been eight or nine at that time."

"That's young for a career decision." It indicated a goal-oriented personality. Probably self-sacrificing, too. Interesting. "So is your grandmother still alive?"

"Oh, no. She passed away years ago. But, with the help of physical therapy and a strict diet, she was able to live about seven more productive years. She was a wonderful woman." A pause. "What about you? Do you have family?"

Court fell back on his cover story. "No. I was an only child, and my parents were killed in an accident some years ago."

"I'm sorry."

Conversation waned and Court relaxed again beneath the kneading ministrations of her hands as the scents of the warm oils she used on his body lulled him. Nice, he thought drowsily.

"There!" she said a moment later. "All finished for this evening. The oil has been absorbed by your skin, so you don't need to shower again unless you're going out or something. It won't negate the benefit of the massage."

"All right." He rose, wrapping the towel firmly

about his hips only to discover that Heather seemed
to be studiously avoiding looking at him. He studied
her profile curiously for a moment. "Thank you."

"For what?" she asked. Was there a breathless
tone to her voice?

He frowned. "For the massage. What else?"

"Oh, I'm sorry I was thinking of something else."
She still avoided looking at him as she began gath-
ering her supplies. "Of course…you're welcome."

For a moment, he actually thought she might be
disturbed by his partial nudity, but he discarded the
notion almost immediately. She was a therapist and
a masseuse, after all. Nudity would hardly bother
her, would it? Writing off her apparent unease to
mental distraction, Court's thoughts moved forward
to their next workout session. "I have an appointment first thing tomorrow morning. But I'd like to
meet here to exercise my leg again as soon as it's
over. Say ten-thirty."

"Certainly. You're paying me to be available at
your convenience."

Once again, that wicked part of himself latched
on to her words, twisting them, weaving an enthrall-
ing fantasy around them. Damn! His mind seemed
to have gone into the gutter the minute Heather Buchanan had walked into his house. Or, perhaps the
associates he'd been spending time with were finally
getting to him. He cleared his throat. "Good. Then
we'll get in two exercise sessions tomorrow."

She nodded. "I don't see why not. Ten-thirty. A
break for lunch. And then again at two-thirty or three
would be good."

He nodded. "Oh, did anyone speak to you about breakfast?"

She shook her head. "No."

"It's not structured, so you're free to help yourself to whatever you find in the kitchen. There's always a pot of coffee on, and Liz usually has some muffins or bagels made. There should be some fruit in the refrigerator, too, if you prefer."

"That sounds fine."

He nodded. "Good night, then." He took a step toward the door and stopped. Now that the therapy was over, incongruously, he found himself loath to leave her. Which meant he should definitely get out of there as quickly as possible.

It was after eleven when Court left the bar and returned to his car, getting into the back seat. He saw a large brown envelope on the floor where Edison had surreptitiously dropped it. Despite his impatience to see what Edison had discovered about Heather Buchanan, Court didn't bother opening the envelope. He'd do that in the privacy of his study when he got home—just in case there were prying eyes in the night.

Having spent a good two years setting up the current sting operation, there was no way he would jeopardize that in even the smallest way. Not if he could help it. Especially not when there were only weeks left until all their hard work paid off. Just a few weeks, and then he could get back to his own life.

At midnight, Liz came into his study with a carafe of camomile tea and a couple of cups. She'd taken to doing that when she'd learned he wasn't sleeping well. Setting the tray down on the corner of his desk, she turned to close the doors and then asked, "So, what did you find out?"

"Preliminary investigation says she's just who she claims to be." Court shifted a few papers, scanning the information, and then read, "Heather Marie Buchanan, twenty-eight, was employed by the Northwest Hospital up until two weeks ago, now works at the Rockford Clinic. She lives with her younger brother, Desmond Buchanan, age nineteen, still in university." He looked up. "She lied about that. Makes you wonder why, doesn't it?" Without waiting for a response, he returned his gaze to the report. "No brushes with the law for either of them so far. At least nothing that came up in the search."

"Parents?" Liz asked.

"Both deceased. Have been for ten years."

"How?"

"Doesn't say." He frowned. "I'm going to have Edison do some more digging. I've still got the feeling that something's not right here."

"Me, too. But, you know…I like her."

Court nodded. "I know what you mean, but that could just make her more dangerous. Edison left a note to say that he's circulating her picture to our people to see if any of them have seen her. So far, nothing."

At that moment there was a discreet knock at the door, and Ernest poked his head in. "Court, I think you might want to see this."

"What?"

"The security cameras in the hallway of the bedroom wing show little Ms. Buchanan in the starring role of snoop. And she just made her way into your room.''

Court's face darkened as he leapt to his feet. ''Damn! I hate being right all the time.''

Minutes later, he stood in what they called the ''control room''—actually just an extra bedroom— simultaneously viewing the surveillance screen showing his closed bedroom door and the rewind of the tape of Heather slipping surreptitiously down the hall. He watched as she checked over both shoulders before hastily turning the knob and slipping into his room.

The evidence was pretty damning. Heather definitely had ulterior motives for being here. He glanced again at the current surveillance screen just to assure himself that she was still in the room, then looked grimly at Ernest.

''So, what do we do?'' Ernest asked.

Court shook his head thoughtfully. ''My first instinct is to confront her, find out who she's working for, then get her the hell out of here. The problem with that scenario is that it's reliant on making her talk. And from what I've seen, Ms. Buchanan is pretty good at thinking on her feet. She might refuse to tell us anything. And we *need* to know what's going on here.''

Ernest nodded. ''Agreed. So…we watch her.''

Court nodded. ''Like a hawk. She's got to meet with someone sometime. And then we'll know who's behind planting her. Once we know that then, hopefully, we can determine the motive. It's unlikely that whoever it is really *knows* anything or they would have moved on us more decisively.''

Ernest nodded. ''I hope she meets with him soon, whoever it is. We don't have a lot of time.''

Court nodded solemnly. ''And keep your fingers crossed that there hasn't been some kind of a leak. At this stage of the game, that could prove disastrous.''

''Yeah,'' Ernest agreed sourly as he turned back to the screens. Still no sign of Heather.

Heather quietly closed the medicine cabinet in Court's bathroom. He wasn't on any prescriptions that she could see. With the exception of the most common headache medication, some antiseptic and gauze, the shelves were empty. She examined the surface of the vanity. He seemed to like a fairly large variety of colognes and used an electric razor.

Big deal!

There had to be something here that would satisfy DiMona's demand for information at least temporarily. She moved back into the bedroom. She'd done a quick examination of it when she'd first entered the room and hadn't even found Court's identification—so, tonight he must have been carrying it on him. Still, perhaps there was something she'd missed.

The room, done in shades of royal blue and gold, was neat and tidy. Mrs. Kaiser's doing, Heather surmised. There wasn't so much as a shoe or a shirt out of place. So where should she look? She'd checked the polished walnut dresser and bureau. She'd checked the nightstands. And, she'd checked under the bed.

Darn it anyway! She couldn't spare much more time without risking getting caught. Nerves had her checking over her shoulder to make certain that the door to the room remained closed.

The closet again? She hadn't really given it a thorough search. Maybe she'd better check it more carefully.

Her decision made, she opened the closet doors and dragged a chair over so that she could stand on it to check the top shelf, continuing her search. Jeans. A stack of sweaters. A camera. An umbrella. A…wait a minute. What was this?

She picked up a small black book and flipped through it. An address book. Only there were no names and addresses in it. Frowning, she studied a few of the entries. Each one had two or three letters which could have been initials followed by, in most cases, a ten-digit number. Phone numbers? Possibly. But the numbers had been run together in one long number. Strange!

Still, it could be something.

Taking out the pen and small pad of paper she'd brought along for just this eventuality, Heather hastily recorded a few of the entries. Then, replacing the address book, she hopped down off the chair. Quickly setting the room to rights, ensuring that she'd left no evidence of her entry, she made her way to the door, opened it and peered cautiously into the hallway.

All clear. But she wouldn't heave a sigh of relief

until she'd made it safely back to her room in the next wing of the U-shaped house.

She was just turning the corner when she collided with something solid, or rather someone. As her heart all but leapt out of her chest, she made a choked sound that barely contained her terror and raised her gaze to meet Court's hard amber eyes.

Oh, no!

"Heather!" he said, raising a brow in surprise as he grasped her arms to steady her. He glanced beyond her, into a corridor in which she had no business being, before looking back at her. "Are you lost?" he asked.

She gulped a breath and stepped back, out of his grasp, as she groped desperately for a response. "No. No, of course not. I was just—" she paused, waving an arm in the direction from which she'd come "—checking to see if I could get to the pool from this wing. It would be closer."

"Hm," he returned, scrutinizing her in that way that made it seem he could look into her soul. Then, reaching out one long-fingered hand, he smoothed a tendril of hair off her cheek, tucking it behind her ear. "You know, Heather, sometimes people get lost and don't realize it until it's too late to even attempt to retrace their steps. I wouldn't want that to happen to you."

Her face tingling from his gentle touch, Heather stared at him. What was he talking about? Aloud, she said, "Right. Well, um, thank you." Stepping around him, she escaped down the hall, all but racing to her bedroom door as she replayed his cryptic comment in her mind. It sounded vaguely like a warning.

Slowly, she reached up to touch the spot that still tingled from his touch.

It felt like an assault on her senses.

Chapter 5

A night and a day had passed since Court had learned that Heather Buchanan was indeed in his household under false pretenses. Now, Court lay in bed staring into the darkness. Yet he could find no real reason for his insomnia. Unable to sleep, his thoughts turned to his therapist. Although he had yet to learn definitively what her true purpose here was, he could surmise a couple of scenarios—neither of which was good for him.

And, because of his inability to drive as of yet, the decision to follow Heather wherever she went necessitated bringing in another person—because Ernest could well be with Court when Heather left the house. Rather than being additional hired help—which might be stretching the budget a bit even for a lawyer of his supposed stature—Dave Pirello was going to be Ernest's nephew, here to visit his uncle and help out where he could. In his first year with the DEA, Dave was young, idealistic and eager. According to Edison, he would be arriving tomorrow morning.

As his thoughts returned to Heather for the umpteenth time, Court found himself wishing that he didn't like the woman so much. She'd actually yelled back at him during their afternoon exercise session. He liked that. He hadn't met a woman who could stand up to him since he'd left home.

Home.

God, he missed it sometimes, the ranch, his family. His little sister, MacKenzie, who was not so little anymore. She'd been a beautiful young woman the last time he'd seen her, a researcher and information broker who stayed tied to the world via her computer despite her physical isolation in the wilds of Montana. Heck, she seemed to know more about what went on than some of the politicians in Washington. He worried about her sometimes, though. About her solitary existence and the way she'd withdrawn from men. He hoped that someday, despite her heartache, she'd find the man who was right for her.

Then there was his younger brother, Chase, who still slaved away on the ranch in Montana that they'd grown up on, and loved every minute of it. Had the backbreaking work helped him to heal? Court wondered. The murder of Chase Morgan's young wife, Rayna, had been the talk of Flint County for a long time. Probably still was. And yet, in the two years since it had happened, not a single clue had surfaced that would have helped them solve it. Court had even taken time off of work to do a little investigating of his own just after it had happened, but it hadn't helped. He wished he'd been able to find something, some way to ease his brother's mind, his pain.

With a sigh, Court threw back the bed covers and sat up, gouging at his eyes with thumb and forefinger as he muttered an earthy curse. He was tired, but it wasn't the tiredness that came from lack of sleep—though there had been precious little of that lately. Rather, it was a bonedeep weariness generated by having heard and seen too much.

Rising, keeping his knee locked, he limped to the window, seeking a distraction, any distraction to draw him from the monotony and pain of his own thoughts. He found it when he noticed the lights on in the solarium.

Strange. It was after midnight.

A minute later, he caught a flash of emerald green and saw a lithe female body, silvered by moonlight, slice the water. Well, well. It looked like Ms. Buchanan was having trouble sleeping, too. Maybe they'd be better off not-sleeping together. He really didn't like the idea of her wondering around the house alone again. Not that there was much to find, but still he needed to know the truth about why she was here.

Heather was biding her time until she was certain the house was asleep before going on a midnight sleuthing expedition. She was supposed to contact DiMona the evening after next, and so far, other than the cryptic data she'd copied from the address book the previous night, she had almost nothing to give him. She'd hoped the swim would calm her, prepare her for what she had to do. It hadn't. Now she dried herself, rubbing at a few tendrils of sodden hair that had escaped the clip on top of her head, and tried to focus on what lay before her. She needed to get into Court's study.

"Having trouble sleeping?"

With a startled cry, she whirled in response to the deep masculine voice, coming out of the shadows.

"I'm sorry. I didn't mean to frighten you."

"I... It's all right." Swallowing, she draped the towel around her neck and watched Court advance across the blue-patterned tile floor of the solarium. He was wearing a royal-blue bathrobe, left to hang open, over a pair of red boxer-style swim trunks. At least she thought they were swim trunks. "I just wasn't expecting anyone else to be up." Not to mention the fact that the sense of guilt she was already feeling was making her jumpy.

"I was having trouble sleeping," he said by way of explanation. Not that he owed her one. "Thought I'd have a nightcap. You want one?" He moved toward the bar in one corner of the solarium and leaned his cane against the wall near at hand.

She shook her head. "No, thanks."

He raised an eyebrow as he withdrew a crystal decanter of amber liquid from behind the bar. "It'll help you sleep."

"I've never learned to tolerate hard liquor. The occasional glass of wine is my limit."

"Ah, I have an excellent vintage right here." Replacing the crystal decanter, he reached to extract a bottle from the wine rack.

"No, really—"

"It'll help you sleep," he reasserted, interrupting her and proceeding to remove the cork from the bottle. "I'll join you in drinking it, okay?"

Heather observed him for a moment. She couldn't very well do her exploring now anyway, and the wine would help her sleep. "Fine."

He flashed a brief smile. "Good."

As he set out the glasses and poured, Heather found herself incapable of taking her eyes off him. Or rather, off the disturbing expanse of hair-roughened chest that he'd left exposed. No man had the right to be so…compelling. Had she lived in the days of old, she might have wondered if he was a sorcerer capable of beguiling her with spells and potions. Being a modern day woman, she just wondered instead if she might be dealing with the devil in disguise. How else could she explain the effect this man was having on her?

Oh, he had a magnificent body to be sure; and she should know because she'd seen most of it quite intimately, but…there was something about him, a slight coldness at his core, a ruggedness, that prevented him from being handsome. It was almost as though he stood outside himself watching the actions and reactions of those around him with a detachment that few people had. And sometimes, like now as she met his dispassionate gaze, she had the strangest sense of kinship with a bug under a microscope.

"Come and join me, Heather." Carrying two glasses of red wine, he indicated a pair of deck chairs and then proceeded to set the wineglasses down on a patio table before taking a chair himself.

Heather took the towel from around her neck, spreading it on the seat of the fabric deck chair to keep it dry, before sitting.

"You don't have to do that," he protested. "The fabric is designed for poolside use."

"I don't mind."

He nodded and passed her a glass of wine. It felt awkward sitting here like this with him—two strangers in semidishabille who happened to be sharing living quarters. Heather felt his gaze move over her, as tangible as a caress. "You look nice in a swimsuit."

"Thank you." She flushed and, to disguise it, quickly sipped her wine though he probably wouldn't be able to see her heightened color in the muted solarium light anyway.

"So, Heather, have you lived in Seattle long?"

She nodded. "About ten years I guess. Ever since I was eighteen. I moved in from Redmond to go to school."

"Hm. Twenty-eight and not married. Ever come close?"

She shrugged, her mind skirting away from dreams long abandoned and pain undiluted by the passage of time. "Yes. Once. A long time ago."

"What happened if you don't mind my asking?"

She did mind, but she knew it was time she moved beyond her pain, so she forced herself to respond. "He was killed," she murmured.

Court frowned. "I'm sorry. Car accident?"

Heather shook her head and then sipped her wine for courage. "No, he—he was a cop." A lump formed in her throat and she found herself forcing the words past the constriction in a way that was physically painful. "He was shot during what he thought was a routine traffic stop."

Court's voice seemed to gentle. "How long ago did it happen?"

"Six years." She stared wistfully into her wine. "He was a wonderful man. Kind. He—" She broke off.

"He…" Court prompted when she didn't speak again.

She sighed. "Let's just say that Jay took me under his wing and helped me to deal with a difficult situation that I'm not certain I would have gotten through without him."

Court sipped his wine and considered her. "And there's been nobody in your life since Jay?"

Heather shrugged. "Nobody serious. I was too busy raising my—" She broke off suddenly as she realized that only yesterday she'd stated that she had no family ties.

"Your what?"

She cleared her throat and hastily took another sip of wine, giving herself time to think. "My level of qualification in physical therapy. Working toward my masters degree."

He nodded, but said nothing. Heather received the impression that he didn't believe her, although, in truth, there was no way to tell. His expression was as enigmatic as ever.

Unable to sit still any longer beneath his observant gaze, she set her wine on the table and rose to walk to the wall of the solarium where she could look down on the myriad twinkling lights of Seattle. "It really *is* a beautiful view," she commented a moment later.

"Yes." His voice, husky, strange sounding, came from just behind her, startling her. Turning, she found that he wasn't looking at the view of the lights at all, but at her, and his predator's eyes glowed with an almost feral light. Her heart leapt into her throat. Oh, no! Even as unpracticed as she was in the exchanges between men and women, Heather recognized that look. She'd seen it before—a long time ago—and remembered its seductive power.

As his potent gaze imprisoned hers, her breath hitched in her throat. If only he wasn't standing so close, maybe she could think more clearly. "I—I think I'd better turn in for the night." That was what she needed to do. Escape.

He nodded, but made no effort to step out of her way. "Do you know how beautiful you are?" he asked in a low voice.

"I..." Heather didn't know how to respond.

He seemed to sense her unease. "I'm sorry. I didn't mean to make you uncomfortable. Too much wine." He offered the excuse with a heart-stopping, intensely appreciative glow in his golden eyes. "Moonlight, red wine and a beautiful woman. It's a heady combination."

With an effort of pure will, she pulled her gaze from his. He was too serious, too intense. And she was drastically out of her depth. "I'd really better turn in. Good-night." She began to sidle past him.

"Heather?"

"Yes?" Wary, but tantalized despite herself, she lifted her eyes once more to meet his. It was a mistake. As though the gesture had been some kind of signal, he gently grasped her arms—his hands like hot irons on her water-cooled skin—and slowly drew her toward him. She felt curiously fragile beneath his hands. A shiver raced through her in the wake of his touch. She told herself it was just the contrast between the warmth of his palms and the coolness of her own skin that had caused it, but she wasn't certain she believed it. She could only stare up at him in mute surprise as he slowly drew her into a tender embrace. Imprisoning her within the circle of his arms, he lowered his head to capture her lips with his. There was no hesitation on his part. No awkwardness. And Heather found herself seduced by the confidence of his touch, the warmth of his body.

Her nipples, flattened against the hard surface of his chest, tingled and tightened. Her lungs seemed to contract, and she had difficulty breathing. He made a sound deep in his throat. Satisfaction? Desire? And increased the pressure of the kiss slightly.

Molten heat spread through her limbs. No! Heather tried to deny her response, to exert some control over it. But her will crumbled beneath the onslaught of a desire made more powerful by abstinence. With a soft sound of protest and surrender, she opened her lips to him.

His response was immediate. He tightened his embrace until she felt every contour of his hard chest against her swollen breasts. He deepened the kiss until she felt consumed by its fiery heat. He pressed her against the solid evidence of his arousal until her knees turned to rubber.

It felt so good to be held by a man again. To know

that for just these few seconds, in his arms, she was safe. Cared for. She had been alone for so long, reliant only on herself. And now, Court's strength and power were every bit as seductive to her as his touch.

No! That wasn't right. Court could well be the enemy. And if he was, she would have failed Des again. *Des!* She couldn't forget her purpose here. Not even for a moment.

Wrenching her head to the side, she broke off the kiss and took a desperate step back. "No!" Instinctively, she raised a hand to protect herself from the gentle but devastating assault on her senses, but her slap never connected for he blocked it with ease. Grasping her wrist gently in his large capable hand, he stared down at her, his golden eyes gleaming in the muted combination of moonlight and underwater pool lights. Heather found herself answering the unspoken question in his eyes. "I'm sorry. I can't. Please…just let me go."

He stared at her for a moment. "Forgive me."

Heather nodded, but her senses were still too befuddled to attempt a response. She was vaguely aware that his hands grasped her shoulders, caressing the contours he found there as though attempting to ease the tension knotted in the muscles, but she was more aware of the sensation than of the action itself. And the sensation frightened her with its subtle power to beguile.

And then suddenly, as his fingers traced the shape of an old and telltale scar high on her back, his hands stilled. An instant later, his massaging thumb found the scar's mate, in front, beneath the strap of her suit just a couple of inches below her collarbone.

"Heather?"

Her breath arrested in her lungs. She knew what he was going to ask, and she had no idea how she was going to respond. Certainly not with the truth. It would raise too many questions. "Yes?" she managed.

Stepping back, he stared down at her with that astute topaz gaze that wrought such havoc on her senses. Then reaching out with his index finger, he moved the strap of her suit aside and touched the scar again sending a jolt of awareness shooting from the point of contact to the tip of her nipple.

His voice, when he spoke, was little more than a seductive whisper, but it held an underlying core of steel that was unmistakable. "How exactly does a physical therapist go about getting herself shot?"

Oh, Lord, he knew! She hadn't realized he'd be so certain. And yet she couldn't tell him. She wouldn't. It was not something she spoke of. She'd learned long ago that the past belonged in the past, and she kept her eyes firmly fixed forward—on the future. Admittedly, her future might not be too bright at the moment, but she had no choice. She'd simply have to bluff.

"Shot?" she repeated incredulously. "I wasn't shot." She touched the small scar herself. "This is from a skiing accident."

He studied her for a moment, his gaze revealing nothing of his thoughts. And then he said, "I see. And what kind of skiing accident would do that?"

"Landing on a broken ski pole."

"Ah," he nodded. "Of course. I should have realized."

Did he believe her or not? She couldn't tell. "Well, I think I'll turn in." She backed away a couple of steps. "Good night."

He nodded. "Good night. See you in the morning."

Court watched her walk away, her lithe form sensuously graceful in the muted light of the solarium. "Ski pole, my foot," he muttered when she was out of earshot. Another lie. And he had yet to learn why. What was her purpose here? Who precisely had sent her? With only six weeks left until the operation reached its conclusion, Heather Buchanan was an unknown quantity that he couldn't afford.

Chapter 6

The morning exercise session was a study in ignoring tension. Heather was trying desperately *not* to remember what it had felt like to feel his lips on hers. To keep her concentration on completing her assessment of Court's condition for DiMona.

"Let's start with the parallel bars," she said as soon as he finished his session on the exercise bike. "I need to see you walk. Try to walk as naturally as possible without depending on the bars for support, if you can." The morning was only half over and, under his watchful gaze, every second seemed to drag. Unfortunately Court had had no appointments that morning, so there would be no reprieve.

"Sure," he said.

Immersing herself in her work, she observed him for a couple of minutes as he made his way back and forth. For the most part, he was able to avoid using the support of the bars, but he compensated by keeping the knee of his injured leg rigidly locked. "Does it feel like you're walking naturally?" she asked.

"Pretty much. Yeah," he responded.

She looked for a mirror and spotted one. "Come and look in the mirror." She waited while he did as she'd bidden, and then pointed out his firmly locked knee. "Look at the difference between your knees. Can you relax this one at all?"

He frowned and slowly relaxed the knee.

"You're not putting any weight on it," Heather observed. "Try sharing your weight evenly between both legs."

He did as directed. His leg wobbled slightly, and Heather reached out to steady him, to lend her support should it be necessary. It wasn't. Forgetting herself, she looked up into his face and smiled. "Headway. It's supporting you even while in a slightly bent position. So, the leg has already begun to regain some strength."

His gaze dropped to hers, golden-eyed and predatorial, yet his tone when he spoke was low, a bit labored and somehow almost intimate. "Yeah, but not fast enough," he said. "It feels like I'm trying to balance two sticks together end to end." Heather's heart leapt as his rich burgundy voice caressed her nerve endings and she was suddenly very conscious of her proximity to him, of her hand beneath his tautly muscled forearm. Of his body heat and the faint scent of his perspiration.

Feeling a flush rise in her face, she quickly looked down. "Yes, well, that's why I'm here, Court."

They proceeded with a series of exercises that ended with him sitting on a bench, shaky and sweaty from exertion. "Okay, last one for this morning," Heather said as she fastened the Velcro tab of a light weight in place on his ankle. "We're going to try something a little different. Can you slowly straighten the leg?"

The muscles just above his knee leapt in response, but nothing happened. She looked at his face, saw the strain. "Can you kick toward me?" she asked.

He swore. "Does it look like I can kick?"

"All right, Court. Tell me what's happening."

"Not a damn thing!" he yelled suddenly, giving voice to his frustration. "Can't you see that?"

She ignored his outburst. "Can you feel any kind of response in your leg?"

"No! It's like a piece of deadwood. There's nothing there. No reaction."

"The kick function isn't working," she murmured thoughtfully. "I guess that explains why you haven't been driving." He wouldn't be able to move his leg between the gas and the brake.

"How do you know I haven't been driving?"

Heather froze as DiMona's words echoed in her brain. *He's not even driving himself anywhere these days, so if you're smart you might be able to figure out a way to make yourself useful to him when he goes out, too.* Had Gabriele's inability to drive been in his file? It should have been, but she wasn't sure. Maybe for some reason Court had left that out of his discussion with his previous therapist.

Shrugging as casually as possible, Heather said, "I think one of the staff at the clinic mentioned seeing you arrive with a driver." Was that a plausible explanation? She hoped so. "Now then, move forward so that you're sitting on the edge of the bench," she directed, changing the subject and praying that he wouldn't notice.

He didn't move, and once again Heather was forced to make eye contact. His topaz gaze was fastened on her, but there was no expression on his face, nothing to indicate what he was thinking.

She cleared her throat. "Court? Can you move forward please? And don't put your feet on the floor. Just let your legs relax."

After a seemingly endless moment, he nodded and his gaze slid away from her face. Dismissing the incident, Heather concentrated once again on the job at hand. There was a definite difference in the appearance of his thighs when there was no support beneath them. "Look here," she said, brushing her hand along the outer side of his injured thigh. "See how it appears slightly smaller or sunken in comparison to your other leg."

He nodded and glanced at her warily, as though preparing himself for bad news. "Yeah. What about it?"

"The muscle isn't functioning the way it should. This one, on the outside of your thigh, connects to a tendon in your knee joint. I think it could be a large part of your problem with stability."

"Okay, so how do we fix it?"

Heather frowned. "I'll have to give it some thought, see if I can come up with some exercises for tomorrow that may isolate and help strengthen that muscle. In the meantime, you might as well shower. We'll try some more massage stimulation this evening after dinner.'' She paused. ''Did you want to exercise again this afternoon?''

He shook his head. ''No. I'd like to, but I have some things to do so I won't be in this afternoon.''

Heather nodded, wondering if what he had to do would be of interest to DiMona. Her forehead furrowed slightly as she contemplated just how to go about discovering Court's plans.

''Is something bothering you, Heather?''

She started. ''Oh, no, not at all. I was just thinking that, if you're not going to be needing me this afternoon, I should go out and get a couple of things done myself. Do you mind?''

He shook his head. ''Of course, not.'' He began walking toward the door. ''Just let Mrs. Kaiser know before you go out if you're planning on being here for dinner.''

''I will. Thank you.'' Heather had no idea what she was going to do with her free afternoon, but she had a half-formed notion that perhaps she should follow him, if she could.

Court halted in the doorway. ''Oh, if you see a strange young man wondering around the house, don't let it bother you. Ernest's nephew, Dave, is going to be visiting for a while.''

At exactly three o'clock, Court entered the history section of one of the local bookstores. There was a man already present, perusing the American history shelf behind Court. A moment later, he brushed past Court with a muttered ''excuse me'' and left. Court browsed, slowly making his way around until he faced the American history shelf. He picked up a couple of books on the Civil War and replaced them after a cursory glance. Then, ensuring with a casual scan that he was not being observed, he opened a book on "The Battle of Antietem", removed the brown envelope that had been left for him, and hastily placed it in an inside pocket of his jacket.

Now, he'd go for a cup of coffee and a pastry and see what Edison had come up with.

Entering the coffee shop, he ordered and then, balancing his tray on one hand while he used the cane for support with his other, he moved to a vacant table to sit back to back with the man who'd brushed by him earlier. He prepared his coffee, took a bite of the pastry and then opened the envelope.

The DMV records for Heather Marie Buchanan were on top and he scanned them before flipping through the other sheets: a copy of a certificate proclaiming her competency as a physical therapist, a record of employment from the Northwest Hospital and a birth certificate. A typewritten report stated that she'd been living in Seattle for about 10 years, having moved from Redmond and that her brother was currently a resident of the Rosewood Rehabilitation Center. Interesting. The last thing he came to was a photograph. It showed Heather emerging from the Bayside Emporium, an import-export business known to be under Colombian control.

Damn! Just when he was starting to like her. Aloud, he murmured, "This isn't coincidence?"

The man at his back responded from behind his raised newspaper. "There are no coincidences. Remember? We haven't connected her to any particular person yet, but we're viewing her appearance as suspicious. Watch her.''

Court frowned thoughtfully as he gave the appearance of continuing to peruse the papers while he sipped his coffee. Then he spoke again. ''She has an old scar on her left shoulder. A bullet wound.''

Silence. Then, ''That's not good.''

''Tell me about it. Check it out, will you? There should be a hospital record somewhere.''

''Mm-hm.''

Court stuffed the papers back into the envelope, finished his pastry and coffee and then rose to leave.

Heather surveyed the myriad cars coming and going and parked along the street, but it was no use. She'd lost him. Damn! She simply was not cut out for the spy business. Now what was she supposed to do?

She pulled into a parking spot with a sigh of frustration. Well, she'd lost him, and that was that. She might as well spend her free time doing something else. Something important.

It was time she went to visit Des. She missed him desperately, but had been avoiding seeing him for a couple of reasons. The first was that she didn't know how to tell him what she was doing. He wouldn't want her putting herself at risk for him. And the second was that she hadn't wanted to make anybody who didn't already know of his existence aware of him.

But her free afternoon could best be spent with her younger brother.

Her decision made, Heather put her Volkswagen

in gear and pulled away from the curb. She didn't notice the silver sedan that pulled out a few cars behind to follow her.

A half-hour later, she pulled into the visitor parking lot at the Rosewood Rehabilitation Center that had become Des's temporary home. It hurt to come here. Hurt to know that, in some way, she had failed her younger brother. Hurt to think of Des dependant on drugs supplied by people like DiMona, manipulated by DiMona. But if it hurt her, then how much worse must Des feel? He blamed himself.

Consumed by her thoughts, she didn't notice the silver car that parked a couple of spaces away.

A few minutes later, she was standing in the doorway of Des's empty room, trying to determine just how to find him, when a man wearing black jogging pants and a white T-shirt sporting a Red Dog logo emerged from the next room.

"You looking for Des?"

She nodded. "Yes. Do you know where he might be?"

"Probably the TV room. It's 'round the corner, second door on the left. I'm goin' there now. Want me to tell him you're here?"

She shook her head. "No, that's all right. I'll just walk with you, if you don't mind?"

The man shrugged. "Sure."

As they walked silently, along the corridor, Heather retreated into her thoughts once again. How was she going to explain to Des that she wasn't living at home, without revealing to him exactly what she was doing to safeguard his life? She'd just have to bend the truth a bit, that's all. She'd have to say that she was hired by a wealthy client to work exclusively with him. That would probably work. For the time being at least.

Upon entering the TV room, she spotted Des immediately. He looked better. Much better than he had the last time she'd seen him. And, he looked more like their father every day. Whereas Heather had inherited their mother's auburn hair and hazel eyes, Des had inherited their father's black hair and brilliant green eyes. Had they not shared many similar features—high cheek bones, straight nose, firm jawline—and had it not been for the few freckles that dusted Des's nose, people might have argued that they shared the same parentage at all.

"Heather!" He smiled and rose the second he caught sight of her. Rushing toward her, he swept her into an embrace. Des had never fallen prey to the normal teenage awkwardness concerning affection toward family members. Perhaps because all they'd had for more than ten years now was each other.

Returning his enthusiastic hug, she smiled and said, "Hey, Bro. How are you?"

He smiled. "Better now."

Dinner that evening passed at a snail's pace—or so it seemed to Heather. Ernest, Dave and Liz Kaiser had gone out, so she and Court were alone in the house. A situation she would rather have avoided. She would have given almost anything to avoid Court entirely, and not tempt fate—because every moment she spent in his company increased her unwelcome attraction to him. But with DiMona's directive that she find something on Court within a week hanging over her head, she knew there would be no escape. The problem was that Court, himself, seemed a bit preoccupied this evening and thus far she'd been unable to penetrate that wall with any of her questions.

Twirling the stem of her wineglass, she sought again to open the conversation. "So, Court, where do you call home? Where were you born?"

"Pennsylvania. Lived there all my life until I went to law school."

"And after graduating…that's when you moved to New York?"

Having just taken another bite of his dinner, he nodded, but said nothing.

"So, what motivated you to become a lawyer?"

"It wasn't a calling, if that's what you mean. I wanted a job that offered me a decent living, and I didn't have any desire to follow my parents into the medical field." Picking up his wineglass, he allowed it to dangle from his fingers as he looked at her— seeming to truly see her for the first time that evening. "And, to be honest, I enjoy it and seem to have a knack for it." He smiled. "But, that's enough about me and my ordinary, oh-so-boring life. Let's talk about you for a change."

"Me?" Heather asked. "I've already told you everything there is to tell."

"Oh, I doubt that."

Heather considered him, her throat closing as she wondered if there was a double meaning to his words. She said nothing, seeking desperately for a way to turn the conversation around.

"Who is the real Heather Buchanan?" he asked. "The woman beneath the professional exterior?"

"I don't know what you mean."

"Sure you do. What matters to you Heather? What do you enjoy doing? What are your hobbies? What do you dream?"

Heather swallowed, nodding as she began to understand what he was after. "All right. Well...my work matters to me, helping people. I enjoy cooking and hiking. I love nature, and I'd love the chance to go camping again someday. I haven't been in years."

"So, you're a country girl at heart."

She shrugged. "I've never thought of myself that way, but I suppose you could say that without being too far off the mark."

"What about dreams?"

Heather studied her wineglass with singular concentration. Dreams were for dreamers. And she didn't dream. Not anymore. Because dreams didn't come true, and there was nothing more painful than the shard of a shattered dream. But she couldn't say that, so she simply shook her head and said, "I don't have any."

"Everyone has dreams."

Heather shook her head. "Not me. I think it's best to accept life as it comes, to value each moment, you know? Because if you concentrate too much on achieving some nebulous dream, you miss out on life."

Court studied her for a moment as though absorbing the nuances of her words. "That's a pretty astute observation. Not many people are so perceptive unless they've received a lesson in their own mortality." His gaze shifted to her shoulder. To the exact spot where the scar lay concealed beneath the thin fabric of her dress. "Staring death in the face can do that."

Staring death in the face. Yes, Heather had done that. Once. In a time that only escaped the walls of her memory in nightmares. Her breath caught and she forced herself back to the present. "Really?" She shouldn't have allowed herself to be drawn into a conversation about herself. It was dangerous, and he was damn good at getting to the core of the matter. "That's unfortunate, isn't it?"

"Mm," he murmured noncommittally. "Other people say that a life without dreams is stagnant."

"Oh, I didn't mean that a person should be completely without dreams. Just that they should not allow themselves to be so consumed by them that they miss the simple joys to be found every day." He studied her again as though trying to read her expression. "So," she said, before he could come up with another question, "what do you dream of?"

He leaned back in his chair. "That's a good question. Mostly I think I dream of having the chance to escape civilization for a while. The life of a hermit looks extremely attractive at times."

At that moment, the phone on the kitchen wall rang. Court rose to pick it up. "Gabriele residence. Marc, how are you? Tomorrow evening? Sounds fine. Tell Mr. Aponte that I'll be there. DiMona? Yes, of course, we've met. All right. Thank you."

The minute she'd heard DiMona's name, Heather's heart had all but stopped. Now she was hyperventilating, unable to catch her breath. A panic attack, that's what it was. She'd never had one before, but she knew the symptoms.

"Heather, are you all right?"

Slowly, she got a grip on her emotions and nodded. "Yes. Yes, I'm fine. I just…choked on a sip of wine."

He resumed his seat and sat observing her with his perceptive gaze. Then he said, "Ms. Buchanan, would you do me the honor of being my date for a dinner engagement tomorrow evening?" He held up a hand as though to forestall an expected denial. "I know it's sudden, but it would be just as a favor to me. No strings attached. It's a black-tie affair at the home of an associate of mind, Gilbert Aponte. I don't imagine you know him?" She shook her head, and he continued. "Anyway, I'm afraid there is no one else available to accompany me on such short notice."

Heather wanted to scream and run. The last thing she wanted was to be in the same room with DiMona while Court was there to observe the interplay. What if she messed up? Gave herself away? She opened her mouth to say that she was sorry, that she couldn't possibly make it. But, only two words emerged, "Of course." She barely heard them over the pounding of her pulse in her ears. Lord, help her.

Chapter 7

As Court dressed for dinner the next evening, he pondered Heather's situation again, trying to work out in his mind what her connection to the Colombians might be. Who exactly was she working for? Aponte? Vargas? Based on her reaction to his invitation last evening, there was no longer the shadow of a doubt in his mind that she *was* connected to them in some way, which was precisely the reason he'd asked her to come as his date rather than the DEA agent who had been put in place for that purpose. Heather was legitimately a physical therapist, so she wasn't working undercover with the local cops. The most likely conclusion was that she was probably, in some capacity, working for the Colombian's counterintelligence man, Rick DiMona—on whom the DEA had virtually nothing. Yet, she really didn't seem the type.

Okay…so did DiMona have something on her? Was he blackmailing her? How? The brother?

Court frowned. Dave had reported following her to the rehabilitation center yesterday…after she'd attempted to follow Court and lost him. He had to smile at that. There was little question in his mind that she was a rank amateur. Still, that could make her even more dangerous.

A little checking had revealed that Desmond Buchanan was still a resident of the Rosewood Rehabilitation Center. So, the kid had problems, and those problems had to do with drugs. Put the Colombians and DiMona into the pot and stir, and you got a coincidence stew that smelled like trouble. Since Court didn't put much faith in coincidence, instinct told him that what he had was trouble.

So, perhaps the most important question to ponder at the moment was, *why?* Why had *they*—or DiMona—sent Heather into his house?

If Court's cover had been blown, he was reasonably certain that he would have been hit. His superiors had already been scared once—when Court had had his accident. But a thorough check had revealed that the drunk who had run Court off the road was just what he seemed. A loser, to be sure, but he'd had no drug connections, and none to the Colombians. So, since accidents really do happen and it was much too late for anyone to take his place, Court had stayed in position and was working to recover as quickly as possible. Now though, he had reason to wonder again if, in some way, he had inadvertently placed the operation in jeopardy.

If indeed Heather was working for the Colombians—and no other scenario made sense—either they just suspected something, cop or competition, and didn't want to mess up a good contact without proof. Or, they believed Court was who he said he was, but didn't trust him and wanted someone in the house as a safeguard to watch him against the possibility of a double-cross.

Damn! Court needed to know which it was and soon. If the operation was in jeopardy, two years of work could be down the drain. Not something to be taken lightly.

Precisely why he wanted the opportunity to observe Heather and DiMona together in a room. He hoped to gain some insight into whether or not they did indeed share a relationship, and, if so, what kind?

Heather stared at herself in the mirror in her room. She wore a simple black sheath dress, unadorned, with black high-heeled sandals on her slender feet. She had washed her long hair, curled it slightly, but left it loose. Now, the glass reflected the image of a glamorous stranger back at her—revealing none of the terror that rippled through her system in waves. How had things gotten so out of control? If she had thought herself in the lion's den in Gabriele's house, where would she be when she joined him for the dinner that would include DiMona?

The sensation that the situation was spiraling out of control, unfolding beyond all hope of management, intensified. What if she failed?

No! She wouldn't fail Des again. She could do

this! After all, she'd found the courage to face Herrera and DiMona in the first place.

As though the meeting had been only yesterday, she could still feel Herrera's dispassionate gaze on her as she'd sat before his desk at the Emporium. Still sense DiMona lounging against the wall at her back, breathing down her neck. Still hear Herrera's callous words. "Are you nuts, lady?" Rising, he'd propped his fists on his desk and leaned toward Heather as though his proximity could somehow impress upon her the stupidity of her proposal. "Do you know who I am? What I do?"

Swallowing the nausea in her throat, Heather had forced herself to ignore her queasy stomach and trembling hands. "Yes, I know what you do."

Herrera was a drug dealer. Unfortunately, he was the drug dealer from whom her immature and unthinking younger brother had stolen ten thousand dollars.

"So what the hell gave you the idea that I might consider a repayment plan?" Herrera demanded. ":Do I look like a friggin' banker? Or, is somebody out there spreading a nasty rumor that I'm a nice guy?"

Before Heather could respond, DiMona had interrupted, his autocratic tone eradicating any illusion that Heather had had that he was simply Herrera's body guard. "Wait a minute, Herrera." And then DiMona had turned his sharklike gaze on her. "Didn't I hear the kid mention once that you're a nurse or therapist or something?"

"I'm a physical therapist."

And suddenly, for the first time, Rick DiMona

smiled. The gesture sent chills down Heather's spine. "Now, isn't that a coincidence? That's just what we need."

Was it a coincidence? Heather wondered now as she clenched her fingers into fists to still their trembling. Or had she and Des been played like a pair of fiddles? She'd probably never know. But somehow she had to get through this. Taking a deep breath, she smoothed a nonexistent wrinkle from her dress and turned to leave the room. Court would be waiting.

"You look beautiful," he said as she neared where he waited in the foyer.

"Thank you," Heather managed to reply. She felt like she was going to her own funeral.

Court helped her on with her coat, freeing her hair from her collar in a way that sparked little shocks of awareness all up and down her spine as his fingers brushed against the sensitive skin at the back of her neck. His touch created fissures in the icy wall of her terror, prompting her to become aware of him, of his devastating allure. He wore a black suit and snow-white shirt that complimented his dark looks perfectly.

"Shall we go?" he asked. The small diamond stud he wore in his earlobe winked in the light.

She nodded, and he grasped her elbow to lead her out to the car. Ernest was driving, so she and Court got into the rear seat. It wasn't a limo, but the luxurious interior certainly made it feel like one.

Once they were under way, Heather tried to force herself to relax. She found Court's presence at her side oddly comforting as the blackness of the night enfolded them, but she still didn't know how she was going to get through this dinner without falling apart. She dreaded her first sight of Herrera and DiMona, with his soulless eyes.

As though he sensed her turmoil, Court reached across the chaste amount of space separating them to enclose her icy fingers in his large warm hand. "Nervous?" he asked. Was his tone subtly mocking? Or was it her imagination?

Heather looked at him, but the harsh planes of his face remained characteristically expressionless, revealing nothing in the muted light. She took a breath, reaching for calm. "A bit," she acknowledged. She refused to fall into the trap of trying to explain. Besides, anybody would be entitled to a little nervousness on a first date, wouldn't they?

Thirty minutes later, the car turned into a wide gated drive, and, after the briefest of stops, was waved through. The house they approached was an enormous English Tudor, complete with circular turret on one corner. A stone balustrade, echoing the stone on the house's facade, surrounded a tiled front patio that led up to a pair of cedar doors. The place was absolutely stunning, but Heather found herself incapable of awe at the moment.

As Court grasped her arm to lead her toward the house, her stomach knotted into a fist and refused to ease.

"Heather—" Court said in a low voice.

She looked at him. "Yes?"

"You're as white as a sheet. Is something wrong?" This time there was no mistaking the slightly taunting inflection to his question.

Heather's spine stiffened. Did he suspect something? "Of course not." She shook her head and swallowed as she racked her brain for a believable explanation. "Just nerves. I—I'm not used to this kind of thing. If they go in for tons of silverware, I may not even know what fork to use."

"Ah," he said. "I know what you mean."

"You do?" She looked at him in surprise.

"Mm-hm," he returned without elaborating. "Just relax and follow my lead. I won't abandon you."

Yeah, right! The knot in her stomach didn't ease.

"And I promise I won't let anybody eat you," he assured her.

Heather stared up into his oh-so-serious face and realized that he was actually teasing her. She forced a smile to her lips. "I'm completely reassured."

"Ah, yes. I can tell."

The minute they entered the house, Court noticed DiMona standing off to one side observing the guests. He saw DiMona's gaze flick over the almost nonexistent bulge in his jacket, taking note of the shoulder holster he wore before dismissing him and turning his attention elsewhere.

It was interesting to watch the Colombian's counterintelligence man at work. Exquisitely beautiful women rated scarcely a glance from him, unless they made an abrupt move that attracted his attention. The drone of conversation went unheeded, unless a loud or angry word caught DiMona's notice. Yet, he took inventory of every perfectly tailored suit jacket with a telltale bulge signifying a shoulder holster, and noted every booted foot that might conceal a knife.

Nothing escaped the man. Part of that was no doubt due to his training as a cop, but part of it was pure instinct.

The fact that DiMona was aware that Court was armed didn't bother him. Romano had once told him that they'd run into stockbrokers and lawyers in the past who suddenly took to carrying guns when they began associating with Aponte's people. He'd laughed about it, saying that if push came to shove and they ever actually drew their weapon, they were usually shaking so badly they couldn't hit the broad side of a barn. And, since DiMona had never seen Court draw his gun, as far as the Colombians were concerned Court was just another lawyer carrying a gun to give himself courage. It was what he wanted them to think.

Snagging a couple of appetizers from a tray presented by a passing waiter, Court guided Heather around the room stopping to chat here and there as he, too, used his powers of observation. His instincts told him that it was going to be an interesting evening.

The dinner was interminable. As luck would have it, Heather found herself seated directly across from DiMona. She kept wondering when he would approach her. She was positive that he would: tonight was the night she was supposed to have called him with the information she'd garnered on Court anyway. And she had nothing to tell him.

Well, not nothing, exactly. But she sensed that what she'd learned was not the kind of information DiMona was looking for.

"You're not eating."

She started slightly at the male voice so close to her ear and met Court's observant gaze. "I—I'm really not hungry."

"So it would seem. I don't think you've taken a bite."

Heather didn't know what to say to that, so she said nothing. She could feel DiMona's interested scrutiny on her, and her skin crawled.

"You should try it, Ms. Buchanan," DiMona said. He smiled, revealing far too many teeth, reminding Heather once again of a shark. Everything about the man was cold, mechanical and deadly. "The prime rib is excellent."

Heather nodded and forced herself to meet his eyes. "I will. Thank you." She barely managed to suppress a heartfelt sigh of relief when a man farther down the table spoke to DiMona, drawing his attention.

She wondered who the man was. A drug dealer? A killer? Or a simple businessman? Would DiMona and his kind actually associate with people who had no idea what they were behind the facade? Probably—if it suited their purposes. She still didn't even know what Court did for them.

Oh, Lord, what was she doing here with these people who wore masks of civility like Halloween costumes? She'd almost allowed herself to forget who Court Gabriele was, and what kind of world he inhabited. He was a compelling man, handsome on the rare occasions when he smiled. He'd treated her well, thus far, and he was certainly an excellent kisser if one could judge by the single kiss they'd

shared. But, he was also a man involved with Colombian drug dealers. Who'd even brought her into
the home of one of them. And now, she sat across
the table from the man who threatened her brother's
life.

She glanced at DiMona again, to find him observing her almost expectantly. What would she tell
him? Would it be enough? If not, where did that
leave Des? She lowered her eyes to her plate again.

As though he sensed her distress, Court reached
over to take her hand in his, to stroke her fingers
absently while he continued his discussion with
Marc Romano across the table. She was startled.
Both by his touch and by the way DiMona's gaze
flicked to their clasped hands as though reading
some meaning into it. Damn it! What was Court doing?

But, despite herself, despite the harrowing situation in which she found herself, his touch sent
awareness rocketing through every fiber of her being.

DiMona gave her a sharp look and panic shot
through Heather hard on the heels of the awareness,
making her heart race. Tugging her fingers from
Court's grasp, she forced a few bites of food past
her wooden lips. Oh, no. DiMona wouldn't hurt Des
if he thought she was interested in Court, would he?
Or would he think she couldn't be trusted? Her
throat closed at the thought, and she almost choked.

Des. She couldn't allow anyone to hurt him.

Eventually, the dinner ended and Mr. Aponte's
guests congregated by the pool, talking and laughing
like guests at a party anywhere.

Desperately seeking a few moments of solitude and silence, Heather excused herself and made her way to the washroom. She stayed there as long as she dared, but when a pair of laughing and joking women seemed to be waiting outside the door, she left. Nodding to the women, she began to make her way back to the pool area where she'd last seen Court.

She'd just passed a grouping of potted palms in a quiet area of the house, when someone grasped her arm.

Stifling a gasp of surprise as she recognized DiMona, battling the instinct that told her to flee at any cost, she allowed him to tug her into the shadows.

"So, what do you have for me?"

Not quite daring to tell him *nothing,* she summarized what she had learned about Court's condition.

"So, he can walk without the cane if necessary?"

She nodded, feeling terrible about violating patient confidentiality. "Yes, but his leg is quite numb, and the strength unreliable."

DiMona nodded. "What else?"

Heather swallowed, wracking her brain for any tidbit while she dug in her evening bag for the small scrap of paper onto which she'd copied the information she'd found in Court's room. "I copied this from an address book I found."

DiMona nodded, scanning the information, and stuffed it into his pocket. "Anything more? Any strange phone calls, or curious conversations with his staff?"

Heather shook her head. "None that I heard."

"What about your searches? Did you turn up anything?"

"There are some family pictures on a wall in the living room. They seem to confirm that he's an only child." She frowned. "Nothing more than the address book in his bedroom."

"What about his office?"

"I haven't been able to get into it yet."

"Computers?"

Heather shook her head.

DiMona stared at her. "You're going to have to do better, Heather."

"I know that, but I'm not a spy, damn it. It's going to take me some time to figure out how to go about this."

"It had better not take too long." He smiled his cold sharklike smile. "And in the meantime, I'll drop by the rehab center and take Des some flowers." He began to turn away, dismissing her.

Heather grabbed his arm. "You stay away from Des. Do you hear me? Just leave him alone."

Taking her hand from his arm, DiMona held it casually in his. "You *hear* me, little lady. Get close to Gabriele any way you can and find out everything there is to know about him. Keep a diary of his comings and goings, who he meets or talks to, what he says to his staff. Hell, I want to know what he eats for breakfast. You understand?"

"I'm not his secretary. I only see him for his therapy sessions and at dinner."

DiMona looked her up and down and then smirked. "I'm sure an intelligent lady like you can figure out how to get closer to him than that.'' Releasing her hand, he stepped away. "If you don't want me to pay a visit to young Desmond, then you'd better get me something I can use. Meet me at the zoo at 4:00 p.m. in five days' time. The monkey cage. You got that?''

Heather nodded and watched DiMona stride away. Then, on shaking legs she made her way back to the party and Court. The man she was supposed to spy on. The only man with whom she felt safe in this den of criminals.

Chapter 8

"Join me for a nightcap in the solarium, will you?" Court asked as they entered the house upon their return home. Although phrased as a question, just barely, it wasn't one.

Court could tell by her expression that she wanted to refuse, but something stayed her. Nodding, she allowed him to lead her into the solarium where the only illumination was moonlight and muted underwater lighting.

One thing he was reasonably certain of was that if Heather was working for the Colombians, she was not doing it by choice. He'd caught her expression in a couple of unguarded moments when she looked at DiMona, and he had seen fear reflected there. She'd known exactly what kind of person DiMona was. Of that, Court had no doubt. And that lent more credence to his belief that DiMona was blackmailing her. But how? And even more importantly, to *him* at least, was *why?* What did DiMona suspect?

Court watched her as he poured them each a glass of wine. She appeared pale and fragile in the moonlight. And once again he felt a surge of protectiveness toward her. Which was absurd. For all he knew, once her machinations were complete, *he* might be the one who needed protecting. Still...

Somehow, since he couldn't get rid of her, he had to get close to her. Close enough that she'd confide in him and tell him what was going on. And in that moment, he realized that he was going to do his best to seduce her. Not a hardship certainly. But risky.

Turning to the stereo behind the bar, he put on some music. The slow-dance kind. Then, as the rich sounds began to flow from the speakers installed throughout the solarium, he carried the glasses of wine over to where Heather stood staring pensively out at the city lights again.

"Thank you," she murmured as she accepted the glass.

He studied her. "You're not very talkative, are you?"

She offered him a half smile and sipped her wine before responding. "Actually, I think it's just that I don't know you well, and I don't know what you like to talk about, because when I'm with friends I'm told I sometimes talk too much."

He looked into her eyes, holding her gaze for a moment, seeking evidence of duplicity. He detected none. "I'd like to become one of your friends, Heather," he said quietly.

She caught her breath as though his words had

taken her by surprise and then stared up at him with wide, vulnerable eyes. "I—I don't know what to say."

He smiled slightly. "Can you use another friend? Or are you up to quota?"

"I think one can always use more friends," she murmured. "If they're the right kind."

"And what's the right kind?"

She looked at him for the longest time as though weighing her words, and then she simply said, "The kind that don't hurt you. A true friend."

"They are not the same thing, Heather. A true friend will sometimes hurt you in order to save you. Like a man who forces his buddy to face the truth and admit that he's an alcoholic."

Heather turned slightly to stare out at the city lights once more. Then she shrugged slightly. "I suppose you're right." Her attitude said that she had dismissed the topic.

So much for philosophical discussions. He'd have to try another tack. "Will you dance with me, Heather?"

She whipped around to stare at him. "But, your leg…"

"My leg will be fine. I'll keep the knee locked."

She continued to stare at him doubtfully. "I guess it would be all right."

She made no move to set down her wineglass so he took it from her nerveless fingers and, moving to a nearby patio table, set down both it and his own glass. Then, after propping his cane up against a chair and abandoning it, he extended a hand to her. Once again he saw reluctance in her eyes, but something must have been goading her on because, after only a second of hesitation, she accepted his hand and moved into the circle of his arms.

He held her loosely, knowing that to rush things would only frighten her. It took time for a woman to become accustomed to a man's touch. Gentleness to keep her from bolting. The problem was that Court wasn't sure how much time he could afford to spend on this particular seduction.

The music swirled around them, and even with his rigid leg, he managed a fairly smooth approximation of a waltz. The scent of Heather's perfume, a slightly exotic gingery scent combined with the more heady scent of jasmine, rose to entice him. He felt the warmth of her body through the thin fabric of her gown. Saw the throbbing pulse in her throat that betrayed her nervousness. Sensed her insecurity, her innocence, in the way she avoided meeting his gaze. And he knew that, whatever her reason for being here, Ms. Heather Buchanan was way out of her league.

But he couldn't let that stop him. Not with almost two years of work and countless man-hours invested in their current operation. And so, as the music swirled almost magically around them, as moonlight bathed them in its cool, silvery radiance, Court lifted her chin with his finger and looked into her eyes. "You're very beautiful, Heather."

Her eyes slid away. "Thank you," she murmured in a rather perfunctory manner. He recognized the tactic. She was trying to keep an emotional distance. And that was something he couldn't allow her to do.

Lifting her chin once more, he studied her face

and then slowly lowered his head to capture her lips with his. Soft, full, clinging lips, as succulent as ripe fruit. She didn't exactly respond to his overture, but she didn't pull away, either, so he pressed his advantage, increasing the pressure on her mouth, running his tongue over her lips until she opened to him.

And an instant later, as he basked in her innocent surrender, he forgot why he was doing this. He forgot everything but the blood thrumming through his veins and the desire pulsing in his loins. She really was beautiful.

The kiss ended, and he surfaced to realize that the music had stopped while the stereo moved to the next CD. It was Heather who reminded him of his purpose. "You're trying to seduce me, aren't you?" she asked, her tone breathless.

He stared at her a moment, startled by her directness. "What makes you ask that?"

She studied him a moment and then said, "I don't know. Sometimes I feel as though I'm dancing with the devil in disguise."

Court watched her expression, wondering what she knew or suspected, but he couldn't ask. Not without giving himself away. "Perhaps I've got a bit of the devil in me," he suggested. "Most people do, don't you think?"

She nodded. "I suppose so." She was silent for a moment, then added, "Some more than others."

The music resumed and Court swept her into a dance again before she could protest. "I'm attracted to you. I won't pretend I'm not."

A blush crept up her cheeks. She was obviously discomfited by the conversation.

Dancing with the devil. What a strange expression for her to use. And yet, in a way, Court understood exactly what she meant. He'd been dancing with the devil for years. That's what you did in undercover work. You danced with the devil and prayed that you didn't get burned. The problem was that the devil wore a lot of masks. Sometimes you didn't recognize him until it was too late.

Court sighed inwardly. He'd gotten so tired of it all. All the subterfuge and the acting. He'd seen too much. Too much pain, too much filth, too much of the devil's domain.

Holding a wholesome young woman like Heather in his arms made him even more acutely aware of the other world that existed out there. Made him long to escape the devil's realm. And perhaps, for tonight, he could—partially anyway. Tonight he could live in the moment. And at the moment, he had a beautiful young woman in his arms. He intended to kiss her senseless, seduce her and to carry her off to his bed. And then—since he couldn't completely escape his work—he would find out just who she was and what she had been doing coming out of the Colombian-owned emporium. Because he couldn't allow himself to forget, for even so short a time, that he had a job to do. He couldn't forget all the lives that could be jeopardized if he was found out. He couldn't forget that at the moment, he was undercover with the enemy.

Now, if only she'd look at him instead of over his shoulder. "Heather—"

She lifted her eyes to his. "Yes?" That was when she saw the expression in his eyes. The intensity.

The desire that bordered on avarice. The resolve that bordered on ruthlessness.

Hastily, she lowered her gaze to a safer place. His chest. No threat there.

But in the next instant, as he turned and his jacket gaped slightly, she knew she'd been wrong. There was a threat, and it struck her with the force of a blow.

Court was carrying a gun! As plain as day, she could see the butt sticking out of the shoulder holster he wore. It was so much a part of him that he'd worn it to a dinner party. So much a part of him that he hadn't thought to remove it before dancing with her. So much a part of him that it served as an icy reminder of the kind of world she'd entered...and hoped to escape as soon as possible.

For the first time in a long time, she found herself thinking about her therapist, Dr. Shaw. At least he'd been right about that much: to get over her terror of handguns and what they could do, she'd had to become acquainted with them. Study them. Reduce them down to the essence of their mechanical parts. Because if you know something intimately, it's often less fearsome. The advice hadn't helped Des, but it had helped her. Nothing Dr. Shaw had ever said, though, had allowed her to get over her discomfort at seeing a gun in the possession of another human being.

But knowing handguns, being capable of using them efficiently and carefully had not eradicated her hate for the weapons. She hated them for their purpose. She always would.

Knowing that, how could she possibly even contemplate a relationship with a man like Court?

Before he could intensify his already potent seduction, Heather pulled out of his arms. "I'm sorry, Court, but I—I can't do this. I just don't know you well enough. Forgive me." Then, before Court could respond, she turned and raced off.

Dumbstruck, Court frowned after her. He felt as though he'd been kicked in the gut. *What the hell did I do?* he wondered. Had those really been tears he'd seen glittering in her eyes? The last thing he'd meant to do was hurt her.

Either his seduction techniques were in serious need of an update, or Heather Buchanan was deathly afraid of becoming intimate with him. Afraid of him. And again he could only ask, *why.*

The next morning Court got his answer when he met with Edison again. The library where they'd chosen to meet was quiet and devoid of people with the exception of three students. He set his briefcase down on the table and opened it to withdraw a sheaf of papers and a brown envelope which he lay next to an identical one already on the table. Then, looking at Edison for the first time, he noticed that he appeared particularly solemn. He frowned inwardly. Whatever Edison had found, it wasn't good.

A muscle knotted in Court's jaw as he began to prepare himself for bad news. He spent a couple of minutes taking random notes and then finally, after a quick glance around, said in an undertone, "So, what did you find out?"

"Everything there is to find out from public records. It's in the envelope,'' Edison responded in a whisper.

"You access medical records?''

Edison turned his head to the left as though looking for someone, and then nodded slightly. "Yep.''

"How did she get shot?''

Edison looked directly at him then, and Court was shocked to see some intense emotion reflected in his eyes. "Read the file, Court.'' Rising, he gathered the books he'd been perusing, along with the envelope Court had brought. "I gotta tell you, she's one hell of a woman,'' he added in an undertone before moving away.

Court stared after him. What the hell?

After a quick glance around to ensure that he remained alone in this secluded corner of the library, Court opened the envelope and set the pages down on top of the open book before him. To casual observers it would appear that he was reading the book.

For long minutes, he sat quietly absorbing the information Edison had compiled. Bureaucratic words on paper that told a story more tragic than he had ever expected. And he realized that he'd misjudged Heather. Despite her aura of innocence, she was not as untouched by the pain and darkness of the world as he had assumed. She had confronted death, and survived.

Shot by her own father!

How could he face her again without revealing the depths of the sympathy he felt?

A bit pensive and preoccupied, Court returned home. He'd go to his study first and put the information on Heather into the safe. Then, he'd have some lunch before his afternoon exercise session. Hopefully by then he'd be able to face her.

Unfortunately, his planning came to naught, for when he arrived at his study, he unexpectedly encountered Heather. She was just emerging from the room. Court paused to observe her as she closed the door behind her with exaggerated care and then glanced in his direction. At sight of him, she jumped, her entire body going into a paroxysm of surprise. He said nothing, merely waited, as he wondered what she would say to explain herself this time.

"Oh, you gave me a fright," she gasped. "I was just looking for you."

He nodded sagely and moved toward her. "Of course you were."

She eyed him uncertainly for a moment. "I just wanted to let you know that I've come up with a series of exercises that I think will isolate the muscle that's giving you the problems with support. We're still on for two o'clock, right?"

"That's right."

"Well...okay. I'll see you then." Turning, she hurried away as though she couldn't wait to make good her escape.

Court decided wickedly to torment her just a little more, "Won't you join me for lunch, Heather?" he called.

She stopped in her tracks and then slowly turned to face him again. "Oh, no. Thank you. I don't think I could eat a thing."

He studied her flushed face with interest. There

was guilt written all over it. ''Fine. I'll see you at two then.''

He observed her as she hurried down the corridor and turned toward the gym. Then he opened the door to his study. Taking one step into the room, he stopped and carefully perused the interior looking for signs of disturbance. Signs that would tell him what Heather had been doing, and, perhaps, for what she'd been looking.

But, a careful examination revealed nothing missing or out of place. Not that he could tell immediately anyway. He'd have to check the surveillance tape. His office was the one room in the house that was under constant surveillance, like the corridors. An evidence-gathering process that was serving double duty with Heather around.

After putting the papers concerning Heather away, he sat at his desk and pondered the situation. He didn't like it. What was she looking for? Something in particular? But the most immediate question was, what did he do about it?

His instincts still clamored to get her out of here. But, he couldn't fire her. He needed her help with getting his leg better. At least until the clinic sent a replacement for her, which they seemed darned slow in doing. Besides, firing her would only tip off those who had placed her in his house that she'd been made, and their next attempt might not be so easy to spot. Damn! This was a mess.

Chapter 9

It was two-fifteen when Heather gave up on waiting for Court to arrive in the gym. Five minutes later, after a brief search of the kitchen, she knocked on the door to his study. ''Come,'' came a muffled voice from within.

Heather opened the door to see Court sitting at his desk with his head propped in both hands.

''Yes?'' he asked.

''I just wanted to remind you about your appointment.''

''Oh, yes. I forgot.'' He rubbed his forehead. ''Can we postpone it until, say three-thirty?''

''Sure, if that's what you want.'' She observed him for a moment. His head was once again propped in his hands while he stared at his desk. His face seemed drawn, there were faint lines of tension that hadn't been there earlier. "Is something wrong, Court?"

He looked up at her and shook his head. "Not a thing, other than one doozie of a headache."

Oh, that was all. She could probably take care of that. Stepping into the office, she closed the door behind her and walked toward the desk.

"I thought we agreed to meet at three-thirty," he said in a strained tone.

"We did. But in the meantime, I'll do what I can to ease your headache."

He shook his head. "That's not necessary. I've taken a couple of aspirin. They should kick in soon."

Ignoring his protest, she walked around his desk to stand behind him. "It's probably a tension headache. And there's nothing better at relieving one of those than getting rid of the tense muscles that cause it." Without waiting for further comment, she slowly began to knead the muscles of his shoulders.

"I don't need a mas— Oh, damn, that feels good."

"I told you."

"Mm," he said, allowing his head to loll forward slightly, "so you did." Heather massaged the tension from his neck and shoulders, in silence for a few minutes, then he spoke again. "There is definite magic in those hands."

She laughed slightly. "I don't know about there being magic in them, but they've always worked for me and I'm rather partial to them."

"I'm getting partial to them myself."

He was flirting with her. The realization sent color

climbing into Heather's face. Maybe it would be prudent of her to terminate this particular massage. "Better?"

"Oh, yeah. Much." Turning slightly toward her so that she sat at a right angle to the desk, he grasped her hand and tugged her around to face him. Then, with his eyes on her face, he lifted her hand and pressed her fingertips to his lips.

The warmth of his lips set her fingers tingling and she tried to gently extricate her hand from his grasp. "Ah, I think I should get back to the gym."

"What's your hurry?" he murmured against her hand. "I'm not even there." Without warning, he rose. Holding her gaze with his, he continued to stroke and massage her hand. "I'm here."

"Stop that, please," Heather said as she tried once more to tug her hand from his grasp.

"Stop what?"

"What you're doing with my hand." She tried to step away from him, but he followed, turning so that she was effectively placed between him and the desk.

"Why?" he asked in a low tone.

"It—it bothers me."

He held her gaze. "Liar. You want me to stop because you like it, and you don't want to like it."

"Don't be absurd."

"I am many things, honey. But I'm never absurd."

Before Heather could get over her startlement at being called honey and think of a response, he tugged her closer. Placing her captured hand behind his neck, he kissed her. Thoroughly.

Her heart stumbled and tilted before righting itself. Her breath hitched in her chest making her feel more than a little light-headed. And a strange kind of excitement coiled traitorously in her stomach. It felt so good, so right. Of its own accord, her mouth opened beneath the demanding pressure of his lips.

She tried desperately to maintain her reason, to remember that Court was the enemy, but the thoughts dissipated like smoke in a breeze. His arms encircled her, clutching her close. Too close. His chest compressed her breasts. His arousal pressed against her abdomen. And her senses swam. Vaguely she was aware of his hand working the buttons of her blouse, of his fingertips on her skin. Warm. Exciting. Tantalizing.

Suddenly an insistent buzzing sound drew Heather back from the depths of passion. The intercom!

"Damn!" Court muttered as he leaned away from her with obvious reluctance to answer the call.

Heather looked down at herself. Oh, Lord, she was sitting on Court's desk with her blouse wide open and the edge of one bra cup pushed down to reveal her nipple. Her face flamed as she hastily began to set her clothing to rights and leapt off his desk. Drowning in her own embarrassment, she didn't even hear the conversation via the intercom.

How could she have lost control like that? How could *he* have taken advantage of her that way? Well, maybe he didn't really take advantage, but…it felt as though she'd been ambushed. Whether by her own emotions or Court's expertise, she didn't know.

Court terminated the conversation on the intercom and reached for her. "Heather—"

"Don't!" She jerked away and walked beyond his reach. "This shouldn't have happened. It *can't* happen. Our relationship has to remain purely professional." She went to the door and then reluctantly turned to add, "I'll be waiting in the gym."

Court stared at the door. He hadn't intended for things to go so far between them just then. If he was honest with himself, he had to admit that he had been carried away in the heat of the moment. And, considering his position, that wasn't good. Still, he couldn't help but wonder what lay behind Heather's emphatic assertion that their relationship must remain a business one. Especially since getting close to him could only further her objective in spying on him for DiMona. It didn't make sense.

He waited a few moments to give them both some time, and then made his way to the gym. As he had expected, Heather was all business.

"Hi," she said. "The first thing I want to try to do is recreate the situation that causes your leg to collapse on you. I think it must be when you rise onto the ball of your foot. That's about the only time that the atrophied muscle would be operating as the primary source of strength."

"Okay." He studied her briefly and found it difficult not to remember what she had felt like in his arms. He cleared his throat in an attempt to banish the recollection. "What do you want me to do?"

"We'll use the parallel bars so that you can control the collapse and catch yourself with your arms if you need to."

Court nodded and positioned himself between the bars.

"Rise up onto your toes." She waited as he complied and then said. "Make sure you're hanging on to the bars firmly, and then shift your entire weight onto your weak leg."

He did as she asked. His leg, although a bit unsteady, supported him. "What next?"

"Unlock the knee. That's the only way to isolate that muscle."

He nodded and bent his leg slightly. It collapsed so quickly that, even holding the bars, he almost fell. It took a moment for him to get his uninjured leg back beneath him and regain his feet.

"I'd say we've definitely isolated that muscle and recreated the situation that causes your leg to fail." Heather smiled.

He looked at her wryly. "You don't have to look so happy about it."

She raised her eyes to his in surprise. "But I *am* happy. Now that we've isolated the muscle, we can work it. And that should hasten your recovery considerably. Depending on how it responds to exercise, you could give up your cane within a couple of weeks." She held up a cautionary hand. "That doesn't mean that your leg will be a hundred percent. The nerve damage will take considerably longer to heal."

"I can live with that. So what now?"

"To begin with, you'll use both legs. I want you to rise onto the balls of your feet and do squats. Make sure you support yourself well. Later, when your weak leg has begun to gain strength, if you want to regain the strength even more quickly, you can try one-legged squats.''

Grimly determined, Court nodded and set to work while Heather observed, correcting his form or urging him on when necessary. She was a good therapist, despite her personal agenda. And that said a lot for her character.

It was eleven-fifty. Heather sat in her room attempting to read as she waited for the time to pass. She planned to wait until midnight in the hope that everyone in the house would be asleep. Since she'd been unable to find Court's notebook computer in the study, she had decided to access the desktop model in the library. Luckily, she was at least semi computer savvy. She had invested in a home computer some time ago to help Des with his studies, and they'd shared it. Hopefully there would be something on the computer to keep DiMona happy.

A few minutes later, she checked her watch again. It was time. She reached the library without incident and slowly opened the door to peek inside, heaving a sigh of relief as she discovered it dark. Closing the door softly behind herself, she took a deep breath, wiped her sweaty palms on her jeans and tiptoed across the room to the computer desk.

So far, so good.

Seating herself at the desk, she turned the machine on and then began to go through the drawers of the desk while the computer went through its boot process. She was busy scanning the labels of some floppy disks she'd found when the machine beeped loudly, sending her heart into her throat. Clutching her chest, she closed her eyes and took a deep breath to calm her racing pulse. Sheesh! She'd never before noticed how loud computers could be.

Plugging a disk into the drive, she checked its directory and frowned. All the files were old. Almost two years old. There was nothing new. She checked two more disks in quick succession. Same thing. Weird! Leaning back in the chair, she contemplated the problem.

Maybe Court simply hadn't backed up his files in a long time. In that case, the files on the computer's hard drive would be the current ones. She used the mouse to click on successive folders, checking the file dates. Same thing. This computer hadn't been used in a long time.

Since the data on this computer was so old, there probably wouldn't be much of interest here to DiMona. Still she supposed she'd better scan some of the files just to be sure.

She'd just clicked on an icon to open a word processing program when a man's voice came from her right. ''Can I help you, miss?''

Heather shrieked.

It wasn't a soft feminine squeak of surprise, but a loud shriek of startlement as adrenaline shot into her system telling her to flee. She leapt to her feet, turned to face the threat only to catch her foot on the leg of her chair. She lost her balance, falling against the man and found herself clutching the fabric of a grey suit jacket as she stared up into the beefy face of the man she knew as Ernest, the butler. Only now, in the darkest hours of the night, Ernest looked nothing like the innocuous butler she'd met during the daylight hours.

His blue eyes looked cold and infinitely suspicious as he stared down into her face. Hastily, Heather pushed away from him as she tried to right herself. Oh, Lord! Was that a gun she'd felt under his jacket? What kind of butler carried a gun in a shoulder holster?

All the terror she'd been feeling in the past few days coalesced into a cold, hard knot of nausea in the pit of her stomach. The lump of fear rose in her throat, and she swallowed. She couldn't afford to let the tiniest bit of apprehension show. Gaining the security of her own feet, shaky though her stance might be, Heather forced a smile to her lips. "Ernest! My goodness, you startled me. Wh-what did you say?"

The butler regarded her in silence for a long moment, then said, "I asked if I could help you find something?"

"Oh, no. Not at all. I was just—" Heather waved toward the computer and sought inspiration "—um, just going to use the computer to write a letter. It's all right, isn't it?"

Once again, Ernest considered her before responding. Finally he said, "I'm sure it is, ma'am, although the software on that computer will probably be somewhat outdated."

"Oh. Is there another computer that you'd prefer me to use."

Ernest shrugged. "Mr. Gabriele has one of those laptop computers, miss. But no one else uses it."

DiMona had been right. Heather nodded. "Of

course. Well, I'm sure this one will do just fine.''
She waited for the butler to leave, but he showed no
sign of departing. "I'll just get back to my letter.''

"Isn't it kind of late to be writing a letter?''

Heather shook her head and lied. "I tend to be a
bit of an insomniac. I find it's better to get up and
accomplish something than it is to lie in bed wishing
for sleep.''

Ernest nodded. "I know just what you mean,
miss. Well, if you need anything, don't hesitate to
call.'' He turned toward the door, and Heather
caught sight of the butt of a weapon beneath his
jacket. It was definitely a gun.

As Ernest exited the room, Heather's thoughts
turned once again to Dr. Shaw. She wondered what
he was doing now. She'd stopped seeing him years
ago when it became apparent that she had healed as
much as she was going to. She was scarred, but
she'd become harder, stronger and certainly less de-
luded about the rosiness of life. Perhaps everything
she'd faced so long ago had been fate, or divine will,
preparation for the trials that confronted her now.

It was another of Seattle's grey, overcast days.
Heather had been in Court's household over a week.
Now, she stood in front of the monkeys' cage, barely
noticing the creatures cavorting within, as she waited
for DiMona to show. She had almost nothing to give
him. A list of the people that she had seen Court
receive in his home office. As much concerning the
comings and goings of Court's staff as she'd been
able to monitor. And, she'd recorded the fragment

of an overheard telephone conversation—one side only, of course. That was about it.

She was under no illusion that what she had to give to DiMona amounted to anything. Where did that leave her in her attempt to protect Des?

Peripherally she noted the approach of a man wearing a beige trench coat, but she couldn't discern any other details. She was about to turn to look at him when he spoke, growling the words in an undertone beneath his breath. "Don't look at me!"

The voice was DiMona's. Heather froze as her heart trembled in her chest. "Wh-why?" she whispered. "Is something wrong?"

"Were you followed?"

Followed! Questions rampaged through her mind. *By whom? Why?* She stared sightlessly at the monkeys swinging around the cage before her. "Wh-why would anyone follow me?"

DiMona swore foully beneath his breath and muttered something about *amateur idiots.* "Never mind. What have you got for me?"

Reflexively, Heather reached for the folded piece of paper in her pocket. "I wrote it down."

"Don't!" DiMona snapped in an undertone. "You can't give it to me here. Meet me in the reptile house in five minutes." Before Heather could respond, he was gone.

Closing her eyes, she drew a deep, shaky breath and resisted the urge to see if she could spot someone following her.

Slowly she turned and began to walk along the path leading toward the reptilian area of the zoo. Surreptitiously she looked around. But, if there ever had been someone following her, he seemed to be gone now.

She didn't see the man standing in the shadow of a nearby exhibit. As Heather disappeared along the path, Court stepped from the shade. If he'd had any remaining doubt that Heather was working for the Colombians, that doubt was now laid to rest.

He trailed after her slowly—not a problem with his leg still uncertain—and stayed out of sight. When she entered the reptile house, he didn't bother following. It would have been too easy to be spotted. For now, it was enough to know that she was meeting DiMona and, undoubtedly, passing on information concerning Court and his activities.

The question he desperately needed to have answered now was why were the Colombians watching him? If they had truly suspected him of crossing them, he had little doubt that he would have been killed. They weren't known for taking chances on people.

Automatically taking note of his surroundings and the people he passed, an ability that had become innate after years of undercover work, Court made his way back to the parking lot where Dave waited in an unobtrusive car. Continuing to ponder the very strange situation he found himself in, he decided he was going to have to confront Heather about her association with DiMona soon.

Damn! Some small part of him had still harbored the hope that Heather's apparent involvement would prove to be a series of coincidences and circumstantial evidence. That hope had just been shattered. He ignored the tightening sensation in his chest that told him that information had come in too late to keep him from getting hurt. Better hurt than dead at any rate.

Chapter 10

"*Heather, c-could you come home? Please?*"
Des's ten-year-old voice was choked with suppressed tears.

Heather was dreaming. Even in the grip of reliving the most horrific day of her life, she recognized that fact. But she couldn't stop it. Couldn't wake up to escape. She could only twist and turn, fighting the spidery strands of the dream even as they gripped her more tightly.

The noise of the diner faded into the background as Heather gripped the telephone receiver more tightly. Des rarely cried. At ten, he considered himself much too mature for such behavior. "What's the matter, Des? Did you hurt yourself?"

"No." He choked back a sob. "S-something's wrong with Dad. He's got a g-gun."

Here's a **HOT** offer for you!

Get set for a
sizzling summer read...

with **2 FREE ROMANCE BOOKS**
and a **FREE MYSTERY GIFT!**
NO CATCH! NO OBLIGATION TO BUY!

Simply complete and return this card and
you'll get **2 FREE BOOKS** and **A FREE GIFT**
– yours to keep!

Visit us online at
www.eHarlequin.com

- The first shipment is yours to keep, **absolutely free!**

- Enjoy the convenience of Silhouette Intimate Moments® books
  delivered right to your door, before they're available in stores!

- Take advantage of special low pricing for **Reader Service Members** only!

- After receiving your free books we hope you'll want to remain a
  subscriber. But the choice is always yours—to continue or cancel,
  any time at all! So why not take us up on this fabulous invitation,
  with no risk of any kind. You'll be glad you did!

345 SDL C26S

245 SDL C26N
(S-IM-OS-06/00)

▼ DETACH HERE AND MAIL CARD TODAY! ▼

Name:	
	(Please Print)
Address:	Apt.#:
City:	
State/Prov.:	Zip/ Postal Code:

The Silhouette Reader Service™ —Here's how it works:

Accepting your 2 free books and gift places you under no obligation to buy anything. You may keep the books and gift and return the shipping statement marked "cancel." If you do not cancel, about a month later we'll send you 6 additional novels and bill you just $3.80 each in the U.S., or $4.21 each in Canada, plus 25¢ delivery per book and applicable taxes if any.* That's the complete price and — compared to cover prices of $4.50 each in the U.S. and $5.25 each in Canada — it's quite a bargain! You may cancel at any time, but if you choose to continue, every month we'll send you 6 more books, which you may either purchase at the discount price or return to us and cancel your subscription.

*Terms and prices subject to change without notice. Sales tax applicable in N.Y. Canadian residents will be charged applicable provincial taxes and GST.

Shock paralysed her. A gun! Where had her father gotten a gun?

"Heather, please come home. I'm scared."

"I'll be right there, Des. Don't worry, okay." She heard her father shout something in the background, and then another choked sob from Des. "I'm coming," she yelled, hoping to reassure him, to distract him. Then, slamming the receiver down she ripped off her apron and raced out of the restaurant without a word to anyone.

The dream shifted.

Suddenly she was home, although she had no idea how she had gotten there. It was untidy, like it had been since the day her mother, Moira, had passed away almost a year earlier. Heather did what she could, but she just didn't have the skill for homemaking that her mother had had. And her father was little help.

Duncan Buchanan seemed to have lost a very important part of himself on the day her mother had finally given in to the cancer that had attacked her. He trailed through each day like the ghost of the man he'd been.

Today though, her father was more animated than she had seen him in a long while. He was pacing back and forth in the living room waving a gun and ranting while Des sat curled up into a tight ball on the corner of the sofa with silent tears tracking down his cheeks.

At first Heather wasn't afraid. Her father had always had a blustery temper, but he'd never been violent. It was when she tried to talk to him that fear blossomed. *"Dad, what's wrong? What's the matter?"*

"Get away from me," he shouted, gesturing crazily with the gun. *"Just shut up and sit down."* Although Heather complied, sitting gingerly on the edge of the sofa, his rage and frustration only seemed to intensify. *"Do you know what they did?"*

"Who, Dad?" she asked in as calm a tone as she could manage.

He didn't seem to hear her. *"After twenty years the bastards. Twenty years! How am I supposed to support my family?"*

It was then that Heather realized that he must have been fired. *"You can find another job, Dad. It's not the end of the world. We'll manage. We always do."* He whirled to face her. Continuing to talk to him, she rose and moved slowly toward him. *"Please…just give me the gun."*

"Gun…" His eyes tracked to the weapon in his hand as though he'd forgotten he held it. And then his expression hardened. *"No. The bastards are gonna pay. I can't let anybody else take care of my family."*

Heather felt tears of fear of hurt and a thousand other emotions burn in her eyes. No! She couldn't cry. She had to be strong, for all of them. Just as her mother had been. And as she often did in times of stress, Heather heard her mother's voice. You will always have the strength to do what needs to be done, child. The good Lord made you strong. And, of course, the fact that you are my daughter helps, as well, *she'd added with an impish grin.*

"Daddy, please stop and think. What will happen

*to us, to your family, if you do something and get
sent to jail? You won't be helping us.'' Despite her
resolve, the tears overflowed and trickled down her
cheeks.*

*As though her tears were shards of glass that cut
him to the quick, his face crumpled. "Oh, baby.
Don't cry. You know your mama would hate me for
makin' you cry. Oh, God, what am I doin'? I'm just
no good without her.''*

*And then, before Heather's horrified eyes, Duncan
Buchanan lifted the gun to his own head. "Daddy,
no!'' Instinctively, she leapt forward to stop him,
grabbing the gun in an effort to tug it from his
hands. There was an explosive noise. A white-hot
pain pierced her shoulder above her left breast. And
then…nothing. Only the sensation of being wrapped
in white, shut off from the world.*

But deep in her dream, she knew what came next
and she fought to escape it. To deny it. "No! No!
No!'' She repeated the word in an endless litany
until finally the strands of the dream lost their power.

Heather sat bolt upright in bed, dashing the tears
from her face in an angry motion. Damn it! A sob
caught in her throat. Ten years! Ten years and still
she remembered every small detail as though it were
yesterday. The nightmare would let her forget none
of it.

Reaching over, she turned on the bedside lamp.
And that was when she saw him. A startled squeak
of surprise escaped her even as she recognized Court
silhouetted in the bedroom doorway.

"Sorry. I didn't mean to startle you. I was passing
by when I heard you cry out.'' Clad only in a pair

of jeans, he carried a steaming cup in his hand. Bare-
foot and shirtless, Court Gabriele was breathtakingly
male.

Heather flushed, wishing she'd locked her door
and saved herself the embarrassment of having her
employer see her in the depths of a nightmare. "It—
it's all right. I'm sorry I disturbed you." In the next
instant, she remembered that she couldn't have
locked her door even if she'd thought of it. Most of
the doors in the house had those old-fashioned skel-
eton key type of locks set just below nonlocking
doorknobs. And, since she didn't have a key...

"You didn't disturb me." He continued to watch
her with those predatory and too perceptive golden
eyes of his. "Are you all right?"

Heather nodded. "Just an old recurring dream."

"Sounded more like a nightmare."

Heather cleared her throat and tugged the blankets
higher. It felt awkward to be sitting in bed looking
up at him. "Yes...well, I'm used to it."

He left his position in the doorway and strolled
into the room. Picking up the chair that sat before
the vanity, he swung it around to face the bed and
sat down. "Tell me about it."

Heather's eyes widened. "Oh, I don't think that
would be a good idea. It's not something I talk
about."

"Why?"

"It's...difficult."

He nodded his understanding. "When nightmares
hold us hostage, sometimes the only thing that will
break their hold is talking about them."

Why did other people always assume they knew

what was best for her? She doubted that he'd ever had a nightmare in his life. "Oh, and you know all about nightmares, no doubt."

For an instant the expression in his eyes grew cold and bleak. Then, to her surprise, he nodded. "Nightmares. Guilt. Fear. Yeah, I know about them." Suddenly he looked at her with a tenderness that she found touching and a bit disconcerting. "Now," he said. "Tell me about the dream. It will make you feel better and I promise I'll never tell a soul."

Still, Heather hesitated. "I don't want sympathy. Sympathy makes me cry, and I hate that."

He held up his right hand. "Scout's honor. No sympathy."

She nipped the inside of her bottom lip in indecision, but something in his gaze reassured her. So finally, for the first time in years she began to try to put her personal horror into words. Her tale was slow at first, stumbling. But gradually as she saw that he was simply listening, not judging, not commenting, the words began to flow more smoothly and she told him about the dream. When she reached the end, she fell silent. Plucking at a piece of fuzz on the bedding, she avoided Court's eyes.

"And you woke up in the hospital?"

She nodded. She and Des had survived that horrible day. Forever scarred perhaps, but they had survived.

"What about your father?"

Heather swallowed and then slowly forced herself to form the words. "He killed himself," she whispered.

Unable to live with the enormity of what he'd

done, unable to cope with what he viewed as his failure to find the means to support his family, Duncan Buchanan had placed a call for help and then, leaving the line open, had put the gun into his mouth and pulled the trigger.

In those few hours, Heather's life changed forever. At eighteen she suddenly had the responsibility of raising her brother. There was some insurance, thankfully, but not enough to make the years that followed easy ones. Heather had worked and paid for the training she'd needed to become a physical therapist. She'd supplemented her training with any other courses that might help her advance and garner a better salary—things like aromatherapy and therapeutic massage.

And, with the assistance of counseling, she had been able to cope with the tragedy and move on.

"How did your brother take it?" Court asked. He didn't bother pointing out that, in her upset, Heather had let slip her brother's existence.

"Desmond didn't adjust as easily as I did," Heather said. "He was younger." She paused, frowning thoughtfully. "He seemed to forget the details, or perhaps he just buried them deep in his mind, but he was never himself again."

"And you blame yourself, don't you?" Court knew about guilt. He knew all about it.

Heather closed her eyes tightly for a moment as though to block out the pain of that acknowledgement. Finally she said, "He called me for help, and I failed him."

"Did you?" Court paused, considering his words. "Did you stop to think that perhaps, in going home, in doing what you did, that you may have saved your brother's life? There's no way to know what might have happened.''

Heather shook her head. "I don't believe that. Dad would never have hurt him."

"He would never have hurt you either, would he?"

"That was an accident!"

"Exactly, Heather. Accidents happen. And the rest of us go on as best we can. There's no shame in that." He rose from the chair and stood staring down at her. "I'm going to go and make you some hot chocolate. I'll be right back."

Heather threw back the blankets, reaching simultaneously for the housecoat she'd left lying across the foot of the bed. "Hot chocolate sounds wonderful, but there's no need for you to bother. I can make it myself."

Court considered her for a moment, taking in the rumpled russet curls surrounding her beautiful face as she belted her conservative but somehow very sexy peach satin wrap. "We'll both make it," he said in a tone that brooked no argument. "Come on."

Court sat sipping his hot chocolate and studying Heather over the rim of his cup. She looked delectable sitting there across from him trying to avoid his gaze. But delectable or not, she had met with the enemy today and he needed to find out why.

"So, Heather, what did you do today?"

Because he was watching her expression closely, he saw the slight flicker of her eyes that betrayed her feeling of guilt. She shrugged, an attempt at non-chalance, but a flush was already climbing into her cheeks. "Nothing much really. A doctor's appointment, some shopping."

Court nodded. If her fair complexion and tendency to blush didn't consistently betray her, Heather would have been a very accomplished liar. "Nothing serious, I hope."

"Serious?" Her gaze fixed on his in wide-eyed perplexity.

"The doctor appointment," he clarified. Well, he amended, maybe not as accomplished as he'd thought.

"Oh." She smiled. "Oh, no. Nothing serious at all." She sipped her chocolate. "What about you? What did you do today?"

"Work," he said. "Not much else." Court had had enough of her incessant questions. So, before she could think up any more he rose and moved around the table to pull her to her feet. "Come with me," he said.

"Wh-where are we going?" Heather stammered, trying to keep her mug from spilling as he tugged her from the kitchen and into the corridor.

"Swimming."

"Swimming? But...it's after midnight."

"What's the time got to do with it? You go and change into your swimsuit and meet me by the pool in five minutes. It'll do us both good to get a little midnight exercise." He could think of another kind of midnight exercise that he wouldn't mind getting, but... Well, the night wasn't over yet.

* * *

Heather stared after Court in surprise as he deposited her at her bedroom door without even considering the idea that she might not want to swim…particularly not with him. Somehow the idea was almost as appealing as it was threatening. "I really don't—" she called after him weakly.

"Be there," he interrupted. "Or I'll be back to get you."

Heather sighed, shook her head and entered her room. She suspected this was one battle she simply would not win, so she might as well capitulate gracefully.

It was closer to ten minutes later and nearing 1:00 a.m. when she hesitantly approached the pool. Soft, sensual music played in the background, seeming almost to be a part of the moonlight and muted pool lighting, but she didn't see Court. Maybe he was late, too. She should go back to her room.

She skirted a deck chair as she peered into the shadows of the dimly lit pool area. Her heart was literally pounding with trepidation. This was pure madness. Foolhardy in the extreme. She needed to avoid Court as much as possible, not flirt with danger. *If you play with fire, you get burned.* The words sounded in her mind as clearly as though they'd been spoken. It had been one of her mother's favorite sayings. A caution from on high? she wondered.

She had just decided to heed the warning wherever it might have come from, and was about to turn back, when there was a faint splashing sound. "Come on in, Heather. The water's perfect." Court's voice drifted to her, dark and beguiling, in the moon-light. Burgundy velvet.

She moved closer to the pool, seeking him in the shadows, then finally saw him surface near the edge, as though he'd come to meet her. "Hi," she said simply, self-consciously, barely managing a smile.

Slowly, agonizingly slowly, his gaze lifted, sliding over her with an almost tangible caress. It moved from her bronze-polished toenails, up her long legs to her hips, over the slight swell of her abdomen, lingered briefly on her full breasts and then, finally, reached her face. "Hi, yourself," he said with a smile. But the expression in his eyes left Heather with little doubt that he liked what he saw. And, unfortunately, she discovered that she very much liked being looked at that way.

Her mouth went dry. She shouldn't be here. It was dangerous. Court Gabriele was just the kind of man she could fall in love with if she wasn't careful, and yet the only thing she knew about him for certain was that he was a man who lived on the edges of society where the violence and ugliness were at their worst. Where the single loud report from a handgun could mean that he would never see another day. Where men like DiMona and his kind thrived. And it was a place that Heather wanted nothing to do with. How could she reconcile her attraction to the man himself with her repulsion for his way of life—no matter who he was?

"Are you coming in?"

Startled, her gaze met his. "Yes." Before she could think about it any more, she dived into the pool and began to swim for the other end.

She sensed him push off the edge of the pool, and begin to swim after her. Within seconds, he caught up with her and began pacing her. He said nothing, merely watched her, waiting for her to acknowledge him. She didn't until she reached the end of the pool. Then she stopped, stood, brushed the mane of russet hair out of her eyes and looked at him.

He smiled. "Race you to the other end and back."

Heather arched a brow. "Oh, sure. This from a man who has the opportunity to practice on a daily basis."

He shrugged. "So I'll give you half a length head start. Are you game?"

Heather grinned. She'd always been a pretty decent swimmer. She might actually have the chance to win this. "You're on!" Without waiting for another word, she dived forward and came up swimming hard.

She reached the other end and pushed off again, noting that Court still hadn't caught up with her. She was going to win! The sheer joy of competition bubbled up inside her. Yes! And then, suddenly, there was a tug on her ankle that pulled her beneath the surface of the water. Coughing and sputtering, she came up just as Court stroked smoothly past.

She reached the pool's edge to see him waiting for her with a cocky grin on his face. "You—you cheat!"

He offered her an unrepentant shrug. "What can I say? I hate to lose. What are you going to do about it?"

Heather stared at him in amazement. "Why you—" Furious, she slapped the water with the palm of her hand, sending a huge geyser into his face that left him sputtering. "That's what I'm going to do about it, you—you—cheater!"

When she saw he was laughing beneath his sputtering, she was infuriated anew and decided he needed more humbling. Using both hands, she began to send consistent torrents his way until he bellowed, "Enough!" between laughs and sputters and began making his way toward her through the torrent of flying water.

Abruptly, Heather realized he was getting too close, and she turned to flee.

"Oh, no you don't!" he laughed.

Grabbing a handful of her hair, he tugged her to a halt and turned her to face him. Then, as she tried to revert to splashing him once more, he lifted her out of the water, foiling her plans. Heather squealed in protest and looked down into his laughing face.

Suddenly though, the atmosphere between them changed, becoming charged with something Heather couldn't name, and as she watched the smile fade from his face she could only wait for what would come. Court lowered her gently back into the water, allowing her water-slicked body to slide over his until her toes touched the pool bottom again. Heather was barely conscious of having regained her feet, for she was held in thrall by the expression in his leonine eyes. It was primitive, feral, and deeply sensual—a force as old as humankind itself—and it called powerfully to something deep within her that she had not known existed. The intensity of that elemental call rocked her to the core of her being, terrifying her with one realization: she could easily fall in love with this man.

Much too easily.

Chapter 11

A small sound escaped Heather's throat as she broke away from him and headed toward the edge of the pool as quickly as she was able. Regret and fear burned behind her eyes in equal measure. Regret for what might have been. Fear for what might yet come to pass.

An instant later, Court joined her. Although she tried to avoid his gaze, he extended a gentle hand, to lift her chin, forcing her eyes up. He seemed to see something reflected there, for his expression grew more solemn. "Is something wrong, Heather?"

She started to shake her head, to deny the problem. *Honesty is always the best policy, dear,* her mother's lilting Irish voice sounded in her mind again, voicing another of the many platitudes she so loved to use. "Yes," she murmured in agreement.

"What?" Court asked.

Startled, Heather realized that he thought she had spoken to him. And he was right to think so. After all, who else would she be speaking to? But now, how did she respond? "I'm afraid, Court."

He frowned. "Of what?"

Heather swallowed, her gaze darting skyward as she sought the words to continue. But now her mother's voice remained obstinately silent. Slowly, reluctantly, she looked again at Court. "You," she murmured. "This—this connection or attraction or whatever it is that keeps happening between us, it's—"

"It's what?" His tone caressed her, burgundy velvet on a sensual sea of moonlight and background music.

She closed her eyes briefly, sending a prayer winging its way heavenward that she wasn't making a drastic mistake and then plunged ahead. "It's dangerous, Court."

His frown didn't alter as he stared at her with his golden-eyed gaze. "I'm not following, Heather. I think you're going to have to be a bit more specific."

He moved slightly closer as though to see her expression more clearly, and the warm water lapped at her breasts. For a second she allowed herself to imagine that the caress had come from him. Then she shook off the fantasy. She had never had time for fantasies, and she didn't have time now.

When she said nothing, he pressed. "How is this attraction dangerous, Heather? What are you afraid of?"

She couldn't meet his gaze. She didn't know what to say.

"Of me?" He seemed confounded.

"Sometimes."

"Why?"

Heather hesitated. She no longer believed in her heart that Court could be a criminal, a killer. In truth, she'd been thinking of him as a cop of some kind for a while now. But…could she be absolutely certain? Sure enough to let information slip that might get her brother killed if Court wasn't the man she thought him to be?

No, she couldn't. So, how could she possibly explain without revealing too much? She could only reveal part of the truth, and that part would be more risky on a personal level than any truth she had ever shared, for her words would reveal the depths of her attraction for him. Something she would much rather keep to herself. If Court was not the decent and ethical man she believed him to be, he could use that against her.

"Remember that I told you I was engaged once, and that he was a police officer?"

Court nodded with a thoughtful frown, obviously wondering where she was going with this.

Heather swallowed, and then plunged ahead. "I don't want to grow to care for another man who carries a gun, Court. And I don't want to risk losing another man I care about to a premature death. A violent death. There has been too much violence in my life."

Comprehension dawned in his eyes. "I see." He

stared off into the night. "So, then, what do we do about this thing between us?"

Heather swallowed the lump that rose in her throat. "We—we ignore it," she responded in a tone barely above a whisper.

He looked back at her then, and Heather almost sobbed at the tenderness shining from his luminous eyes. She had been prepared for many things, anger, displeasure, even hurt, but not understanding. How was it that he could understand her so well? "I'll do my best, Heather," he murmured. "For your sake. But, remember, I'm only human."

She nodded. Then, unable to stay a moment longer for fear that she would burst into tears, she hoisted herself out of the pool. "Good night, Court."

"Good night, Heather." His velvet voice wrapped around her even now, luring her, but she resisted its call and made her escape for another night.

After a near sleepless night, Heather wanted nothing more than to leave. To regain her boring old life. To see Des and make plans for their future. But of all her desires, the only thing she could do was see Des. And *that* she would do, without waiting another minute. Without saying anything to anyone, she wrote Court a brief message telling him that she hoped to be back on time for his 10:30 a.m. exercise session, and left.

Des was reading a fantasy novel when she arrived at his room.

"Heather!" he exclaimed the moment she entered. Jumping off the bed, he rushed across the room to embrace her. "Where the hell have you been?" he demanded. "I couldn't reach you, and I was so worried."

Heather frowned in confusion. "I told you I'd accepted a private position."

He reared away from her to look down into her face. "Yes, but you didn't tell me you'd quit your job to do it. I called, trying to reach you and they said you weren't working there anymore. They couldn't even tell me who you *were* working for." He calmed a bit then, staring into her face with a perceptiveness she wasn't used to seeing from her younger brother. "Sis, what's going on?"

Heather shrugged, avoiding his eyes as she patted his shoulder. "You're being melodramatic, Des. Nothing's going on." She moved toward the only chair in the room. Sitting down, she looked up at him. "Now, sit down and tell me why you were so frantic to get hold of me."

He scowled. "There was no reason. Do I have to have a reason to call my sister?"

"Of course not."

"Good. 'Cause I was just feeling like talking one night, so I tried to find out where you were so I could call you. But the more I learned—or rather didn't learn—the more worried I got. This isn't like you, Heather. Something's going on."

Heather studied him. He was such a handsome young man with his midnight-black hair and bright green eyes. Des should have been out fending off the attentions of amorous young women, dating and having fun. Instead, because of DiMona and people like him, Des was in here, battling the demon of addiction. It wasn't fair. None of it was fair.

Now, she met her brother's determined gaze and swallowed. "Before I explain, I want your solemn promise that you won't do anything stupid," she said. "That you'll stay out of it."

He eyed her grimly. "I don't like the sound of that. I might be able to help, you know."

"Promise me, Des. Or I can't tell you."

He hesitated a moment more and then nodded. "Fine. All right. I promise."

Heather heaved a sigh of relief. Had she seen the crossed fingers he held behind his back, however, she might not have found his promise quite so comforting.

"Now, tell me what's going on," he demanded.

Heather rose to walk to the window where she stared out at the perfectly manicured grounds without really seeing them and proceeded to tell him the truth. "I told you that I had gone to speak to Herrera and that he'd agreed to wait until you were out of here for you to repay his money."

"Yeah."

"Well, that wasn't the complete truth." She told him about the agreement she'd reached with Di-Mona.

When she finished, Des seemed to sag before her eyes. Squeezing his eyes shut, he grimaced, his facial expression mirroring his emotional pain. "Oh, Heather. What have I got you into?"

"Nothing I can't handle," she said, hoping the words were true.

"*Wrong!*" he almost shouted the word. Then

swallowing, he lowered his voice. "Heather these people are ruthless. Once they have their claws into you, they don't let go. And now that you're working for them, they'll keep you working for them." He paused. "Oh, they'll let you think it's finished…until they need you again. But, there will always be another job. Don't you understand that, Heather?"

Heather stared at him, for that was one thing she had never considered. Numbly, she shook her head. "No, Des. You're wrong. I just have to do this and then we'll be free to go on with our lives." Oh, Lord, she hoped she was right. Tugging the strap of her purse more securely onto her shoulder, she suddenly felt the need to escape. To get someplace where she could think. "I have to go."

He grabbed her as she began to turn away. "What did they say would happen if you didn't do what they wanted?"

She didn't want to say anymore. "Please, Des," she begged. "Don't do this."

"Tell me, Sis. Please. I need to know everything."

She closed her eyes and took a deep breath before speaking. "They said that they'd—they'd kill you."

He nodded. "That's what I thought."

"Des—"

He shook off the contemplation and met her gaze. "Yeah?"

"Don't blame yourself, okay? I've been thinking about this, and I think they may have used you to get to me."

He frowned. "What do you mean?"

"I think somebody gave you that false tip about the rigged race so you'd lose that money and be indebted to them."

His expression cleared as he appeared to consider the possibility. She could be right! "Maybe," he conceded. "Where can I reach you if I need to?"

Heather paused a moment before speaking. "The man I'm working with is a lawyer by the name of Court Gabriele, but I think it would be best if you didn't call me there except in a dire emergency. If you want to talk with me and it's not urgent, leave a message in my voice mail and I'll get back to you. You should have done that before. I would have called you and then you wouldn't have had to worry. Right?"

Des nodded. "Sure." Then, he swept his sister into a tight embrace. "Take care of yourself, Sis. I love you."

"I love you, too, hon. Don't you worry about a thing. Your big sister will take care of everything. Haven't I always?"

"Yeah." But that didn't mean that was the way it had to continue to be. Maybe it was time he took a step into manhood and took care of her for a change. At least he could try.

Although Heather wasn't late in returning to Court's, he was already in the gym when she arrived, his body slick with perspiration from the weight workout. He didn't see her immediately, and she watched him complete a set of butterfly presses before repositioning himself on the equipment to use the leg developer. That worried her.

"Court—"

He looked toward her. "Good morning."

Heather nodded. "Good morning." She indicated the weight-lifting equipment. "Please be careful not to stress your leg with weights before we have a chance to do some stretching exercises. You could set back your recovery."

"I already did the stretching exercises and the squats that isolate the muscle."

"Oh." Surprised, she watched him lift the heavy weights of the leg developer. "It's coming along nicely then."

He nodded, straining with the lift. Then on the release said, "Yeah. Still weaker than normal, but…" he strained on the next lift, then completed his statement "…it doesn't collapse anymore."

Heather smiled. "That's wonderful. You'll be giving up your cane then. And soon you won't need me anymore, either."

That realization left her feeling more conflicted than she had imagined. Although she'd been telling herself all along that she wanted to escape, to regain her old existence, she realized now that her feelings for Court had already progressed to the point where it would hurt to cut him out of her life. That realization in and of itself was frightening. Then, she had to consider what DiMona's reaction might be if she was dismissed from her position here before she'd accomplished what he required of her.

"Give up the cane, yeah," Court said in response to her observation. "I've already pretty much done that. Even started driving again yesterday. But—" he looked up at her with a curious light in his eyes

"—you—" he grimaced on the next lift "—I think I might want to keep for another week or so. I still need the magic in those hands of yours."

Heather forced a smile to her lips. A week! Only a week? Aloud she said, "Well, I'll get things ready for your massage, then."

A week! And somehow, within that time, she had to find information on Court that would reassure DiMona and free her from her obligation.

Court finished his workout with a groan that drew her attention. Rising, he retrieved a towel that he draped around his neck and, wiping the sweat from his brow with it, made his way toward her. His walk was completely natural now. The cane that had been so much a part of him when she'd first arrived was nowhere to be seen. She'd known that his condition was improving rapidly, but somehow she just hadn't let herself think ahead to what that meant to her own situation. Until now...

"Heather—"

"Yes?"

"I just wanted to tell you how much I enjoyed your company last night. I had fun."

She studied his expression, seeking deceit, but saw only sincerity. Was this a man who did not base his relationships on the success or failure of his sexual pursuits? "Thank you. Me, too."

He smiled. "Well, I'll just grab a shower and then we can start the massage."

"All right," Heather murmured, watching him as he left the room. She was falling in love. Hopelessly, desperately, impossibly in love. *Heather Buchanan, how could you be so stupid?*

* * *

Later that night, Heather lay in bed, staring into the darkness. It was only ten-thirty, but she hadn't been able to concentrate on her novel so had decided to make an early night of it.

She had one week left to resolve her current situation, and to do that she had to find out once and for all who Court Gabriele was. A cop? A criminal, possibly even a killer? Or, just an opportunistic lawyer? Once she knew that, she could try to plan her way out of this mess. But how could she possibly find out?

She had all but given up on ever getting the opportunity to check Court's ID. He carried it with him all the time except for those occasions when he was exercising in the gym. And in those instances, she was with him and unable to find an excuse to leave long enough to sneak into his room, check his identification and return.

If she slept with him, she'd undoubtedly get the opportunity she needed, but… Well, she just couldn't do that. Besides, to her way of thinking, she wasn't likely to find much anyway. Any cop who was undercover wouldn't risk carrying a badge, would he? Okay, so unless opportunity fell into her lap, checking the ID was out.

That left her with only two things to do. One, locate that damned notebook computer that DiMona was so interested in, and find out what was on it. And, two, spy more actively. Maybe she could find a way to listen outside the door when Court had a client in his study. When the phone rang, she'd have to listen in. And, although she'd exhausted pretty much every prospect in that regard already, she'd try pumping Mrs. Kaiser once more for information about Court's past.

As though to test her new resolve, distantly, in another part of the house, a phone rang. Heather stared at the extension on her bedside table. Could she pick it up without anyone knowing?

Sitting up in bed, she slowly reached over and lifted the receiver from its cradle. "...I wake you?" a man's voice asked.

"No. I was still awake." It was Court's voice.

"Good. Listen, Carrie and I are doing some more planning on the wedding, and I was wondering if you'd be my best man?"

A second of silence. "Well, it's a bit of a surprise, but I'm sure I could do that. What would I have to do?"

"There's not much to it, but why don't we meet for a drink and discuss it?" He lowered his voice to a near whisper. "I need an excuse to escape the planning committee for a while."

Another pause. "Sure. Why the hell not? It wasn't shaping up to be a good night for sleeping anyway. Where?"

"Mario's sound okay?"

"Give me half an hour." There was a click as one of them replaced a receiver. Slowly, carefully, Heather did the same. She felt horribly guilty for eavesdropping, but the guilt was coupled with the conflicting emotions of relief and worry that she hadn't heard anything that would need to be passed on to DiMona.

She lay back down in bed, thinking and watching

the luminous numbers on the bedside clock change. Distantly, she heard the sound of a door closing and wondered if Court was leaving already. If he was going out socially, he probably wouldn't take his notebook computer with him, would he? And, she'd probably never get a better opportunity to seek it out.

Throwing back the blankets, Heather slipped out of her nightclothes and into a pair of black jeans and a T-shirt. Then, after sticking a couple of disks into her pocket in case she found the computer, she crept quietly to the door, listened for a moment then slowly opened it to peer into the corridor. Empty.

She swallowed and took a deep breath to calm her pounding pulse. "Okay, Heather," she murmured to herself. "It's now or never."

She refused to consider what might happen if DiMona wasn't reassured by the information she found. Because that would mean betraying Court. And if she betrayed one man to save another—even her brother—she wasn't certain that she'd be able to live with herself.

But deep inside herself, where it really counted, Heather felt a soul-deep fear so potent that she felt nauseous. For, though she didn't know exactly *who* he was, she sensed that Court was a good man—and, whatever she discovered, it was not going to be the kind of information that would reassure DiMona. Which left her in a no-win situation.

Chapter 12

After glancing quickly in both directions down the corridor, Heather opened the door of Court's study and slipped inside. She stood for a moment, letting her eyes grow accustomed to the darkness before moving across the room to the window where she cautiously drew the drapes.

A moment later, she stood surveying the office in the muted light of the desk lamp. Court's notebook computer was not in sight. Neither was his brief-case—which was odd when she thought about it. He wouldn't have taken his briefcase with him on a social get-together, would he? So where could it be?

She studied the rich oak panelling of the walls. There must be a closet of some kind.

A moment later, she found it. Feeling quite pleased with herself, she pulled it open.

A safe! What good was that going to do her? She

wasn't a safe cracker. As disappointment suppressed her momentary sense of satisfaction, her gaze dropped. At first glance all she saw beneath the safe were shelves loaded with stationery supplies. Then she saw Court's briefcase sitting on the floor of the closet, and, just above it, on the lowest shelf sat a small black object.

The notebook computer! Her foray wasn't a complete loss after all.

Placing it on Court's desk, she sat down in his chair and searched for the latches that would open it. Her experience with a notebook computer was limited to a short test run she'd done on one in one of the local electronics stores one Christmas. She hoped this one wouldn't prove to be too different.

It wasn't. But neither was there much on it, she discovered. It had all the latest windows-based programs, but none of them seemed to have many data files in use. She certainly didn't see any reason for DiMona's interest.

Her head snapped up as a faint clicking sound startled her. It had sounded like the door to the room being closed. But there was no one there.

With a renewed sense of apprehension, she returned to her inspection of the computer. Nothing of interest. A few data files whose identification consisted of a long series of numbers rather than standard alphabetical names. Maybe that's what DiMona was after. Since she couldn't take the time to check out what they were—even if she might have been able to figure it out—she removed the blank disks from her jeans pocket and began to copy as many of the files as she could.

"Hurry. Hurry. Hurry," she urged the computer beneath her breath.

Finally, it finished. With anxiety nipping at her heels like an intractable terrier, she jumped to her feet and replaced the computer in the closet. The briefcase sat there looking tempting, and she knew she should take advantage of the opportunity to check its contents, but she'd been in the office too long already. It wouldn't do to tempt fate.

Right now she wanted nothing more than to regain the relative security of her room.

Opening the door, she checked the corridor.

"Find everything you need?"

With a shriek of surprise, Heather ducked back into the study and closed the door. With a hand to her throat, she leaned against the wall and tried to calm her racing heart.

Ernest had discovered her!

How on earth was she going to get herself out of this? No course of action came to mind.

An instant later, the door to the study opened. Stepping into the room, Ernest turned on the overhead light. "Take a seat, Ms. Buchanan. Mr. Gabriele will be joining us shortly."

Heather blinked at him as her eyes fought to adapt to the now brightly lit room. "Mr. Gabriele?" she repeated numbly.

Ernest nodded and indicated one of the two chairs that sat in front of Court's desk. "Please," he said. "Make yourself comfortable while we wait."

Heather took a step toward the indicated chair and then hesitated. "Well, if you're being thoughtful, I'd be a lot more comfortable in my room."

Ernest considered her. "No doubt. But I'm not quite that thoughtful."

Heather nodded. "I figured as much." Sitting down, she studied Ernest as he leaned his hips against Court's desk and crossed his arms over his chest. He was a big bear of a man, and she didn't stand a chance in hell of getting out of this room unless he wanted her to. Although, if she'd thought it might work, she could very well have clobbered him over the head right then in order to make her escape. The thought of doing physical injury to Ernest was, at the moment, less frightening than facing Court.

Court's mood was decidedly black as he drove back from the meeting at the bar. He'd been informed that the arrival date of the Colombian drug shipment had been moved up. Considerably. In fact it could arrive within the next week or two. They wouldn't know the exact date until closer to the time, but when the word came they had to be ready to move. And that presented Court with a problem on a personal level.

He'd hoped to have enough evidence to charge DiMona with his partner's murder by now, not to mention finding some proof that would stand up in court of DiMona's connection to the Colombian operation. So far he had zip.

And only two weeks at best to find something.

He narrowed his eyes against the glare of oncoming traffic lights. Damn! There had to be a way. Nobody who did the kind of work DiMona did could keep themselves that clean. But, Rick DiMona seemed to have *untouchable* down to an art form.

He went over in his mind everything he knew about the man. Born and raised in Florida, DiMona had had a number of scrapes with the law in his teenage years. In fact, he'd looked to be on a one-way ticket to a life in prison. Then something seemed to have turned him around. He'd entered the police academy right out of high school. That the man was smart had been proven by his grades. He excelled and joined the Miami police force, serving with apparent distinction for a number of years. Until he got caught on the take. He hadn't served any jail time for his crime, probably due to a lack of the kind of irrefutable evidence that would stand up in court, but he had been dismissed from the force.

Unfortunately DiMona hadn't been unemployed for long. With his cop training, he'd made the perfect counterintelligence man. And, in his new job, protecting the interests of the cartel wherever his job took him, he gave free rein to his desire to take revenge on the cops he now hated. The problem was that his involvement in certain cop killings could never be proven. And, if Court didn't come up with something on him fast, it looked like he would walk away once again.

Court swore savagely beneath his breath.

The one thing he had not needed tonight was that phone call from Ernest letting him know that he had an unexpected visitor. Which meant an intruder. It hadn't taken much imagination for Court to come up with the likely culprit, either. If Ernest had apprehended her rather than letting her go, it could only be because he feared she might actually have stumbled onto information that could hurt them if it fell into the wrong hands.

Not wanting to say any more on the cell phone than necessary, Court had simply said, "I'll be right there," and left it at that. Ernest would know what to do until he arrived.

Now, turning into the drive, he winced a bit from the glare as the motion sensors turned on the yard lights. He parked, turned off the car engine and then he sat contemplating the light shining through the curtains of his study. He wasn't quite sure how to handle this situation, and that indecision increased his ire.

Should he let her know that they were aware of her connection to the Colombians? Or, should he allow her to believe that she was still safe in that regard in the hope that they still might learn exactly what she'd been sent to find? The brother was her weakness. Court was certain of it based on the evidence of his drug addictions. But he was just as certain that Heather would in no way risk her brother's life.

But that still didn't provide Court with any inkling as to the course of action he should take tonight. And, since he wasn't going to find the answer sitting out here in the dark, he might as well go in. He'd just have to play it by ear.

He entered the room quietly. Ernest was immediately aware of his entry. Heather sat in a chair before his desk with her back to the door. She flinched visibly when she heard the faint click of the latch as he closed the door behind him. Her shoulders tensed, but she didn't turn.

Slowly Court moved across the room and rounded his desk to face her. Although somehow she managed to keep her face relatively expressionless, she wasn't able to conceal the fear in her eyes. And, since he doubted that she feared him quite that much, there was no question in his mind that, whatever she had at stake in this, it was considerable.

"Good evening, Heather."

She nodded jerkily. "Mr. Gabriele."

"Ah, we're back to Mr. Gabriele, are we?" He'd hoped that, perhaps, their burgeoning relationship and attraction might prompt her to trust him. But it seemed that she'd drawn the line in the sand much farther back than that.

She made no response.

Court observed her closely, reading her body language. "So, Heather. What were you doing in my study?"

She shrugged, avoiding his eyes, as her gaze travelled up and to the right a bit before answering. "I was looking for money."

An obvious lie. "So you're a thief, then."

She seemed to hesitate, as though not quite certain whether she wanted to continue upon the course she'd chosen, and then she nodded. "Of course. What else would I be?"

Court raised a brow. "You tell me."

When she didn't respond, Ernest spoke. "Then you won't mind if we search you to recover any valuables you may have stolen, will you?"

Court looked at him sharply, wondering what he

was about, but didn't have the chance to say a word
before Heather responded. "Search me?" The fear
was sharp in her voice. "But I didn't find any
money."

Ernest folded his massive arms over his chest.
"When I first looked in and saw you, you were using
Mr. Gabriele's notebook computer. I got the definite
impression you were copying files. Mind telling us
what you plan on doing with them?"

Now that *was* interesting. Heather's mouth
dropped open, but not a sound emerged.

"Cat got your tongue?" Court inquired silkily.

"No...um...I..."

"Perhaps I should just have Ernest call the police
and we can move on."

"No!" The panic was back in her eyes. "Please,"
she gentled her tone. "I can explain!"

Now, maybe they were getting somewhere. He
nodded. "Go on."

"Blackmail! I was copying files because I thought
I might find something that would work for blackmail."

Court managed to conceal his disappointment at
her bold-faced lie, but it took effort. Obviously she'd
read a few too many of those mystery novels she
favored. "I fail to see why that explanation should
prevent me from calling the police. Both blackmail
and theft are illegal, Heather."

There was a light of excitement in her eyes along
with the fear now. Adrenaline rush, he concluded.
She was warming up to the roll she was playing.
"But I still have the disks." She reached into her
pocket and held up the objects in question. "If I give

them back to you now, no crime has been committed, has it?''

"The intent was there, Heather. And what about breaking and entering?''

"I currently live here, Mr. Gabriele. Can you be charged with breaking into a room in a house you live in?''

She had him there; it was a grey area. Okay, so she wasn't going to be frightened into telling the truth. Which meant she was more afraid of DiMona than she was of him or the cops. He'd expected that actually, although he'd hoped differently.

Court nodded sharply. "Very well, Heather. I won't call the police at this time. But you've left me with no recourse but to dismiss you." God, he hoped he was doing the right thing. But his hands were tied. What else could he do? "I want you out of here first thing in the morning. Is that clear?''

Heather nodded. "I…yes, of course." She rose and headed for the door as Court and Ernest exchanged looks. With her hand on the doorknob, she turned. "Court—''

"Yes?''

"For what it's worth, I'm sorry.''

It dawned a wet, drizzly day. The kind of overcast day that would stick around for a while. After a sleepless night, Heather rose and left without so much as a cup of coffee or a word to anyone. She couldn't face them. If only she hadn't grown to like them all, perhaps it wouldn't be so difficult. But to see the disappointment, the hurt in their eyes was more than she could deal with right now.

The expression in Court's eyes had been like claws tearing at her heart when he had confronted her last night. The infinite sadness, as though she'd dashed not only his faith in her, but his hope for humanity. His hurt. His anger.

No, she couldn't face him again. In fact, it would probably be best if she never saw him again. She ignored the painful stitch in her chest that that thought induced, writing it off to a sleepless night and stress.

Oh, Lord! What was going to happen now? She still didn't know who Court really was, and that was the one thing DiMona wanted to know most. Would he threaten Des? Her?

If she had slept with Court as DiMona had suggested she do, perhaps this situation would have been resolved already. But she just couldn't. Using her body, using sex in that way, would have left her feeling dirty and immoral. It would have altered the core of her being. And, despite everything, she refused to allow DiMona to have that much influence in her life.

For now, she would go home, have a shower and a cup of coffee, and then she would figure a way out of this. She had to. For herself and for Des.

Heather was so wrapped up in her thoughts that she didn't notice the sedan that pulled out of Court's driveway a short distance behind her. Nor did she notice it following her.

The ground-floor apartment smelled stale after being closed for so long. She opened the windows for some flow-through air before going back out to her car to retrieve her cases. As she was piling the last of them inside the door, she noticed the light on her phone blinking rapidly, signaling that there were voice mail messages waiting.

Damn! She'd forgotten to retrieve messages last night. Her throat closed at the thought that she might have missed something time sensitive from DiMona. With shaking fingers, she lifted the receiver and dialed her voice-mail box.

"Ms. Buchanan, this is Diane calling from the Rosewood Clinic. When Des checked out I forgot to make a follow-up appointment with him. I'd appreciate it if you'd have him call the office. Thank you."

Heather stared at the wall in numb shock. Des had checked out! When? Why? Where had he gone? She looked at the floor by the door. No, there were no size-twelve high-tops in sight. He wasn't home.

She was startled from her daze by the familiar icy tone of DiMona's voice coming through the small speaker, but she missed his words. Swallowing, she replayed the message. "Ellis Park, 4:00 p.m. Naramore Fountain."

Heather glanced at her watch. The appointment was hours away. Maybe by then, she'd have come up with a course of action. Relieved by that much at least, she moved toward the kitchen to start brewing the coffee that she so badly needed at this point.

But where on earth could Des have gone?

She was just stepping out of the shower a few minutes later, looking forward to that first hot cup of coffee, when she remembered her last conversation with Des. But he'd promised he wouldn't inter-

fere. He wouldn't have broken his promise, would
he?

In her heart, though, she knew that, if he'd
thought it necessary to save her, to help her, he
would have. She suddenly got a very sick feeling in
the pit of her stomach.

By three that afternoon, Heather still hadn't found
Des. She'd called all his friends, but none of them
had heard from him. She was frantic. And she
dreaded the coming meeting with DiMona more than
ever, for she feared what he might tell her.

The words *Oh, God. Please, God,* had become a
litany in her mind by the time she arrived at Ellis
Park. Parking her car, she jumped out and began to
wind her way toward the meeting point, completely
oblivious to the beauty surrounding her. Oblivious
as well to the tall, dark-haired man who got out of
his vehicle a short distance away to follow her.

She walked all around the fountain when she arrived, but she didn't see DiMona. Perhaps she was
a bit early. Finding a park bench, she sat down to
wait.

To the man observing her, it was obvious that she
waited anxiously, for she sat forward on her seat,
her spine straight and her shoulders tense. Court
frowned. Was something wrong? He wanted to see
her expression more clearly, but he dared not move
any closer for fear of detection. He shouldn't even
be tailing her himself. That's what they'd brought
Dave in for. But, he needed to. For him, this wasn't
finished yet. It wouldn't be until he knew she'd be
all right.

A moment later, a man wearing a brown trench coat walked by. He didn't so much as pause when he walked by her, and yet something about Heather's reaction to his passing told Court that contact had been made.

Continuing to lean against a wide light standard that provided partial concealment, he glanced over the newspaper he was ostensibly reading and saw her rise to follow.

DiMona then. Had to be.

Cautiously Court trailed after them.

DiMona stood beneath the drooping branches of a cedar, his hands in the pockets of his coat. Heather moved toward him hating that he never took his eyes off of her as he watched her approach. His gaze made her feel exposed…naked.

"What have you got for me?" he asked when she stood before him.

She reached into her pocket, extracting a small sheaf of paper. "I made copies of some calendar notations. Wrote some information about some telephone conversations that I overheard." She shrugged. "That's about it. I was going to bring you some copies of files from his notebook computer but…" She trailed off when she saw DiMona's expression.

"Everything you've given me is next to useless," he growled in a low tone. "I want to know who Gabriele is, and I want to know within forty-eight hours. You got me?"

Heather swallowed. "I'm not sure…"

DiMona pulled something from his pocket and

held it before her face. It was a photograph. "Get sure," he ordered.

Oh, God. Her worst fears had been realized. DiMona had Des!

The photo showed Des tied to a chair. He'd been gagged with duct tape, and yet he stared defiantly into the camera, trying so hard to be brave, trying to tell her not to worry. But she, who knew him better than anyone in the world, saw his fear.

Oh, God! Heather's heart began to pound, the blood to rush through her veins. "No—" But even as she voiced the protest, her vision seemed to narrow. Blackness crept in from the edges as the world around her swayed.

She was vaguely aware that DiMona caught her against his body. She felt him thread his fingers into her hair to cup the nape of her neck. Gasping for breath, desperately seeking stability, she found herself breathing in the scent of his cologne. So normal. Not the way she'd expected him to smell at all.

"There. There. That was a bit of a shock, wasn't it?" He chuckled slightly and she heard the rumble in his chest. In that moment she truly felt hatred. Hatred so potent that it rose like bile in her throat to choke her. Hatred strong enough to make her wish that, just this once, she had a gun in her hand. Hatred strong enough that she wanted nothing more in that moment than to see DiMona dead.

Unable to bear his touch a moment longer, she pushed herself away from him, staying on her feet by sheer force of will. Looking up into his face, for the first time she met his soulless gaze without any fear for herself. "If you hurt him," she murmured. "I'll kill you."

"Threats don't scare me, little girl. Forty-eight hours or the kid buys it." He narrowed his eyes. "And you, too, if you come lookin' for it."

"Bastard!"

He smiled and winked. Backing away a couple of steps, he aimed his finger at her like a gun, clucked his tongue and pulled an imaginary trigger.

Chapter 13

What was she going to do?

DiMona hadn't given her the chance to tell him that Court had dismissed her, and it was probably a good thing. If he'd known that, he might have killed Des immediately.

Des! *Oh, God. Please, God.*

She needed help. There was no longer any question of that. But to whom could she turn? None of her own friends would have the slightest idea what to do. Undoubtedly their advice would be to go to the police. But that would take time, more time than she had. And she couldn't gamble Des's life on making the police understand her situation enough to help her.

Des's friends?

A few of them were probably better capable of

understanding the gravity of the situation, but their willingness to help was by no means assured.

She sighed, closed her eyes and lowered her head. There was no one. Except...

Court?

Was Court Gabriele a cop, as DiMona suspected? If so, if she confided in him, could he help her? She'd gladly spend time in jail if that was what it took to help Des. But...

What if he wasn't a cop? Her instincts told her he was a good man, yet could she place enough trust in her intuition to gamble Des's life on it? To gamble her own life on it?

What choice did she have?

Self-pity is not becomin' to a young lady, Heather girl. Now pull up your socks and face the music. It was her mother's voice again. Even after so many years, Moira Buchanan was still there for her. In her heart and in her mind, guiding her. *And didn't I promise you it would be so? Now go, girl. Do what needs to be done.*

Lifting her head, Heather looked out at the day through tear-blurred eyes and noticed her wet cheeks for the first time. Scrubbing at her face to dry it, she started the car. "Okay, Mama," she murmured.

Stupid! Stupid! Stupid! Court berated himself for the hundredth time as he drove home, negotiating the slick streets a little more recklessly than was wise.

Here he'd been worried about *her.* Hell, he should have been congratulating her on her performance.

He wondered how long she and DiMona had had a thing going.

Well, at least he'd been able to get over his shock quickly enough to do his job. The evidence, two very telling pictures of DiMona and Heather together, could prove quite useful. He shook his head at how close he'd come to missing the shots all together and berated himself anew.

The memory of how DiMona had folded Heather against his body, holding her in a lover's embrace as he threaded his fingers through her hair, replayed again in Court's mind and he cursed foully beneath his breath. Thank God he'd followed her and learned the truth. Otherwise he might have made the same mistake that Brett had.

DiMona had used a pretty woman to get to Brett, too. And it had gotten his partner, his *friend*, killed when she'd betrayed his identity and lured him into a trap. At least Court was still alive.

So far.

Damn! He still had difficulty believing it. And he'd seen it with his own eyes. But there was no question about it; his first instinct concerning her had been right.

Within moments of his arrival home, Court received a phone call from Rachel Fields, his female contact, reminding him of their 7:30 dinner date. The minute he heard her voice, all his senses went on high alert. Something was up! They'd arranged no date. But, they'd given the appearance of having dated casually a few times just to cover this kind of situation.

"I'll meet you there," she said. "I have a few errands to run, so I won't be home."

Pushing all thought of Heather and his own gullibility from his mind, Court had showered, changed, and prepared himself for the *date* which had been arranged at an exclusive sea-side restaurant. But once behind the wheel of his car, despite everything that he needed to concentrate on, Court found his thoughts returning to Heather. Infuriated by the capricious nature of his own mind, he squealed out of the driveway, focusing on the road ahead with desperate determination. Thus it was that he missed seeing the approach of a familiar Volkswagen Rabbit, and didn't notice that it fell in behind him.

"Damn," Heather murmured as she gripped the wheel with white-knuckled fingers, pushing the little Volkswagen to keep up with Court. "Where are you going?" He was speeding, but somehow she had to keep from losing him. This time she couldn't afford to. She managed to keep him in sight, following him through twists and turns and lane changes, even going so far as to run a yellow light—something she never would have done if she hadn't been so desperate—until she followed him to the parking lot of a waterfront restaurant.

He turned another corner ahead, and she pressed the gas pedal a little harder as she tried to close some of the distance between them, then slowed in order to take the corner in pursuit. "No!" She couldn't believe her eyes. In just seconds, he'd disappeared. She was so stunned that she braked in the middle of the street only to be honked at by an irate driver who nearly rear-ended her. "Sorry. Sorry," she muttered absently, still scanning the area for any sign of the BMW. Nothing!

She sped up, taking the corner ahead just to see if somehow he'd been travelling faster than she'd estimated and had turned again. No such luck. Driving around the block, she began a more thorough search of the driveways and parking lots in the area, finally, finding the BMW in the parking lot of a water-front restaurant on her third try.

Studying the restaurant, Heather sat biting her lip in indecision. Though the exterior of the place appeared quite rustic, it was obvious that it was a pretty fashionable place. The waiters wore black trousers, snow-white shirts and black bow ties, and the patrons' clothing seemed to be primarily dressy. Heather looked down at her pleated cream-colored trousers and bronze blouse. She thought she'd pass as dressed for dinner, but it might be best if she simply waited a while. She could speak to Court when he came out.

She parked her car in a manner that allowed her to watch the entrance, then settled down to wait. Thirty minutes later, Heather reconsidered and decided the idea of waiting in the parking lot was not one of her most inspired. She was drawing too many curious glances. Or so it seemed to her. Besides, this was taking too long. She really needed to speak with Court.

Getting out of her car, she headed for the double-doored main entrance, entering the lobby behind a crowd of six or eight people arriving for dinner. Since the hostess was busy with them, Heather took the opportunity to look over the dining room in search of Court. It only took her a moment to spot him seated near the window at the back of the restaurant where he and his companion would have a view of the water. Her eyes flicked to his companion, and widened.

Oh, my! Why hadn't she considered the possibility that Court would have a date? For some reason, she just hadn't. Probably because he'd been alone in his car. She'd made the assumption that he would be meeting a business associate, and she'd presumed it would be a man. It could still be a business meeting, she supposed, but...

As Court reached across the table to squeeze his companion's hand, Heather was surprised by the spark of jealousy that seared her. No, she decided, it really didn't look like a business meeting. It was too romantic a setting for that, she thought as she noted the flicker of the candle on their table. A breeze must have whispered in through the open window at their table. For an instant her gaze returned to that open window. An idea began to form in her mind. But, before it could take shape, she was interrupted.

"Good evening, miss," the hostess's cheerful voice drew her attention. "What name is your reservation under?"

Reservation! She hadn't even considered that. Aloud, she said, "Buchanan. Heather Buchanan."

"And how many are in your party?"

Heather smiled slightly. "Party of one."

"Oh." The hostess's brow arched in not-quite-concealed surprise. Then she bent her head to scan the book on the counter before her. When she didn't find the name, she frowned. "And what time was that for?"

Heather hesitated, uncomfortable with being dishonest, but desperate enough to try to brazen it out. "Seven-thirty, I believe."

"There seems to have been some mistake. I have no reservation under that name."

"That's strange," Heather murmured as she looked across the dining room again. Court and his blond companion leaned toward each other across the table. Whether he had a date or not, she still needed to speak with Court as soon as possible. The restaurant had a roofed porch that was almost empty, probably due to the cooler weather they'd had that day. "Is there any possibility of fitting me in?" she asked. "Perhaps on the lanai?" If she could sit close enough to the open window near Court's table, but with her back to him, perhaps she could overhear enough of his conversation to determine just who and what he was, once and for all, without risking discovery.

And, she'd be in a position to approach him the second the timing seemed right.

"The lanai might be a bit cool tonight," the hostess cautioned.

Heather smiled. "I don't mind."

After a moment's consideration the woman smiled. "Why not? Follow me."

A minute later, Heather was seated exactly where she'd wanted to be. Unfortunately, the noise level was such that she only caught the occasional word of the exchange between Court and his companion.

Still it was enough to keep her intrigued, and she leaned back in her chair to catch as much as possible.

"...shipment...could arrive any time."

"Too soon...be ready..."

"Can I take your order, miss?" Heather jumped, knocking her silverware off the table and almost spilling her glass of water in the process.

She looked up at the waiter in consternation. She hadn't even seen him approach. "I...yes." Quickly scanning the menu, she ordered a Caesar salad with bread sticks, and then resumed her eavesdropping.

She frowned. They weren't saying anything. Risking a glance over her shoulder, she looked at Court's table.

Oh, no! They were gone!

Without thinking, she sprang to her feet and began to scan the restaurant for any sign of Court or his companion.

How could they have disappeared so quickly?

"Lose someone?"

Heather whirled at the sound of his voice. "Court!"

"Hear anything interesting tonight?"

For the first time, Heather noticed that he seemed absolutely furious. His topaz eyes were as hard as the stone whose color they mimicked. His lips had narrowed into a thin line of displeasure. And his features looked as though they'd been carved from granite. "No...I...it wasn't like that," she finally managed to say. "I needed to speak with you, but I didn't want to ruin your date."

"Of course." The sarcasm and disbelief was obvious in his tone. Heather opened her mouth to reassure him, but he didn't give her the chance. "Come on," he said as he gripped her arm. "We're leaving."

She tried to tug her arm from his grasp. "But...my salad." It was a stupid thing to say, and she knew it the second the words were out of her mouth. But there was something about Court and the way he was manhandling her, as though she meant less than nothing to him, that terrified her. She hadn't expected him to be overjoyed to see her, but she hadn't expected him to look as though he wanted to kill her, either.

"You can eat later." Reaching into his pocket he withdrew some money and threw it on the table. And then proceeded to half lead, half drag her through the restaurant.

Heather tried once more to pry his fingers from her arm. "Let me go, damn it!" she demanded in an undertone.

"Not on your life!" He tugged her down the steps and out into the parking lot.

"I have my own car!" Heather argued.

"You won't need it tonight." Opening the door of the BMW he ushered her inside. "I'll send somebody over to get it later."

"But..."

He held up his hand to forestall her argument. "Stay," he ordered as he walked around the car and got into the driver's seat.

"I'm not a damned dog." Heather eyed him resentfully. "And where do you get off treating me this way?"

He gave her an evil look that Heather interpreted to mean that she was lucky she was still alive.

"Court—"

"Look, just shut up, will you? I've got to think. We'll talk later."

"I haven't got time to—"

The look he gave her was enough to give her pause.

"I can wait a few minutes," she said.

His lips twisted briefly in a humorless smirk and then he seemed to forget her existence as he focused on the road ahead with frowning intensity. This was a side of Court that Heather hadn't seen before, and it frightened her a bit. He seemed so intense, so hard.

A few minutes later, they arrived back at his house. Not bothering to pull the car into the garage, Court brought the BMW to a lurching halt before the front doors and got out. Before she had a chance to open her own door, he came around the car, jerked the door open, and said, "Come on," in a tone that brooked no refusal.

Regardless of his mood, Heather decided to try again. "Court, I really need to speak with you."

He paused long enough to look at her. "I want to have a talk with you, too," he said. "But not right now. I have some things to do."

"It's important, Court," Heather argued, as he tugged her into the house.

He nodded. "Yes. It would be, wouldn't it?."

"What?" Heather stared at him in confusion.

He shook his head, leading her through the house until they reached the bedroom she'd occupied up until that morning. Had it really be so few hours

since she'd left? So much had happened, it seemed
like a lifetime. "Make yourself at home," he said
as he ushered her into the room. "You'll be staying
the night."

"Staying the night! I can't—"

He looked at her, his gaze cold enough to freeze
hell, and hard enough to still her tongue in midsen-
tence. She didn't think she'd ever seen a man so
angry. Completely ignoring her protest, he said, "I'll
be with you as soon as I can."

Heather stared after him as he turned to leave the
room, trying to think of something to say…anything,
that would turn this around. But her brain refused to
cooperate.

Abruptly, he stopped, turning to face her. "Oh,
and Heather, I wouldn't recommend trying to leave.
It won't be possible."

Heather was too numbed by his hostility to grasp
the meaning behind his words until it was too late.
What was he saying? That she was a prisoner?

The sound of a key turning in the lock was her
answer. She stared at the door openmouthed. He'd
actually locked her in the room!

Why was he treating her this way? She hadn't
even told him anything yet. She stared at the closed
door in consternation wondering what had changed
in the few hours since she'd seen him last. He must
have learned something from someone, but what?

And would he still help her?

She gazed around the room as though seeking answers, but none were forthcoming. Now what did
she do? she wondered. Having returned all her be-

longings to her apartment that morning, she didn't even have her things anymore.

Frustrated, anxious and frightened—for Des and herself—Heather began to pace the room. A half hour passed and Court still didn't return.

Where was he?

The longer she waited, the more tense she became. There had to be something she could do that would pass the time, and help her relax enough to be coherent when she faced Court. Maybe a quick shower, good and hot, to chase the knots from her muscles. Yes, that's what she'd do. Who knew when Court would decide to let her out of her opulent prison? And when he did, she had to be ready to make him understand.

Court clenched his fists as he moved down the corridor toward Heather's room. He'd just spent a good hour updating Liz, Ernest and Dave on the situation. With the shipment due to arrive anytime within the next forty-eight to seventy-two hours, they had to be ready to move on a moment's notice. And, their circumstances were complicated by the involvement of Heather Buchanan. Even being incredibly optimistic, going on the assumption that she knew no more than she could have overheard this evening, she could probably blow the whole thing. There was little doubt that she could jeopardize the lives of countless people who were just doing their jobs.

"So what are we going to do about her?" Ernest had asked.

"Let me talk to her first, then I'll let you know,"

had been Court's response. He could still see the
incredulity on Ernest's face, even on Liz's. And it
had been then that he'd known for certain that he
was acting out of character. He was jeopardizing
their work for a woman. Unable to reverse course
without providing them with more worry concerning
his competence, he'd simply left it at that. But the
knowledge grated that, for the first time, his partners
didn't fully trust him. And that awareness added fuel
to the already seething fury in his gut.

Because he didn't fully trust himself, he realized.
Because, despite everything he knew about her, he
desired her—in his arms and in his life. Because he
was ripe to believe whatever story she cooked up
because he *wanted* to believe her. He wanted to be
wrong about her. And that was why he couldn't allow himself to be swayed by her.

Pulling his anger around him like protective ar-
mor, he turned the key in the lock and entered her
room. "All right, now what the hell—" He broke
off when he realized that Heather was standing
across the room from him wearing nothing but a
towel. And not a particularly large towel at that. His
heart gave a healthy thud before lumbering to a vir-
tual standstill at the sight of long freckle-bronzed
legs visible beneath the hem of the snow-white
towel. His eyes traveled upward, skimming over the
luscious package hinted at but concealed by the
towel, to delicate bare shoulders, a long neck and a
mass of auburn hair that had been pinned haphazardly atop her head. Corkscrew tendrils, still damp
from her shower, escaped to trail sexily around her
face. She looked absolutely delectable.

Which undoubtedly had been her plan.

Chapter 14

DiMona's coaching? Court wondered.

His anger coalesced into a cold hard knot in the pit of his stomach. Damn her! "What the hell do you think you're doing?" he demanded.

Her eyes widened with an innocence so real he would have believed it if he didn't already know better. "What am I doing?" she echoed. "What are you doing just barging in here? Don't you know how to knock?"

Ignoring her feigned outrage, he stalked into the bathroom, opened the linen closet and grabbed the terry cloth bathrobe that he knew was there. Emerging again, he tossed it to her. "Here. Put this on. Then, we'll talk."

Giving him a fulminating look, Heather turned her back, slipped into the robe and belted it securely. Then, swinging to face him, she threw the towel she'd been wearing onto a nearby chair. "Better?" she asked acerbicly.

Court ignored the question. Just as he ignored the fact that she was naked beneath the concealing folds of the robe, and that his body was reacting to the idea. "Okay. Now I want to know exactly why you were sneaking around the restaurant tonight? Did you honestly think I wouldn't see you?"

He was infuriated by the memory of just how he *had* reacted when he had seen her. His first instinct had been to protect her. Protect *her!* He still couldn't believe it. Yet, he'd concealed her presence from Rachel, hurrying his contact out of the restaurant on the pretext that he had to get moving—all just so that he could shield Heather. Why? But he didn't want to examine that question too closely.

"I wasn't trying to hide from you, just from your date," Heather said. "I was there to *see* you."

He studied her, seeking the evidence of perfidity he knew he could find if he looked hard enough. "Uh-huh," he drawled. "Listen to me, Heather. I want to know the truth about everything. And I want to know *now*. Do you understand?"

She shrugged, allowing the neckline of the robe to gape distractingly. "Where do you want me to start?"

Determined to ignore her blatant attempt at seduction, to remain indifferent to her beauty and the gaping bathrobe, he stalked toward her, perfectly willing to use his size and proximity to intimidate her into providing a candid response. "Start with DiMona. Who is he to you?"

Damn! He'd made a mistake in getting too close

to her. He was close enough for the essence of her to fill his senses. Close enough to be seduced, against his will, by her aura of innocence. Close enough to see the expression in her eyes.

Heather stared up at the big, intractable male facing her. She didn't know how he'd discovered that she had a relationship with DiMona, but it no longer mattered. She'd already decided that she would have to trust Court, trust that her instincts were correct when they told her he was a good man.

As she sought the words she needed to make him understand, all the weeks of carrying her fears and worries alone suddenly caught up with her. ''Di-Mona—'' She stopped as her voice broke and, to her shame, tears filled her eyes for the second time that day. She swallowed the lump in her throat, and forced words past the stricture. ''Dimona is nothing to me. He is the devil incarnate, and I wish he'd go back to whatever hell spawned him and leave me in peace.''

She lifted her gaze to meet Court's, wishing for nothing more than him to sweep her up in his arms and tell her everything was going to be all right. Just for a while, she wanted to lean on someone. Was that too much to ask?

But the expression in Court's eyes remained remote. ''Well,'' he said. ''That was certainly vehement. Hell, it was even believable. Except that I saw you two together today in the park, Heather. I saw him holding you.''

For an instant, incomprehension kept Heather mute. And then as understanding dawned, her eyes widened in horror. ''Good Lord! You think that

I…that he… I would never let him touch me that way. I couldn't!''

"If you're trying to tell me that I didn't see you together, I have to inform you that that tactic is doomed to failure."

Heather dashed the tears from her eyes as anger coursed through her. "Oh, you saw us together, you dolt. But you didn't see what you think you saw. I almost fainted. He caught me, supported me until I stopped swaying. That's all! And even that was too long to be held by him. I would rather have fainted."

For the first time, she saw a slight relenting in Court's expression. The light of speculation that told her he was no longer as certain of his position as he had been. But when he spoke, it was obvious he wasn't ready to give up yet. "Right," he drawled. "I suppose it was heat stroke. In case you hadn't noticed, it was raining today."

Heather squeezed her eyes shut, praying for the means to convince him to help. But as the memory of the picture of Des pierced her mind again, eloquent words escaped her. She opened her eyes to meet his accusing gaze. "He's got my brother!" As fresh tears poured from her eyes, she whirled, preferring to stare blindly out the window than to allow Court to see her so weak, so needy. "He showed me a—'' she choked on the word "—a picture. Des was tied up in a chair with duct tape over his mouth. He was trying to be brave. I could see that. But there was so much fear in his eyes." She caught a sob between her teeth, swallowing it. "That's why I almost fainted. And that's why I was coming to see you. I need your help."

There was only silence behind her. He didn't believe her! If she hadn't been so desperate for his help, Heather would have stalked from the room in fury. But she had nowhere else to turn. "Look, you said you wanted the truth. Maybe you should give me a chance to tell it, from the beginning."

"All right." Taking a seat on the edge of the bed, he indicated that Heather should sit in the chair. "Be my guest."

Self-consciously, Heather sat, adjusting the robe over her legs for maximum concealment. Now that he was giving her the chance to proceed, she wasn't quite certain how to begin. She studied Court's face. It was virtually expressionless, and yet she had come to know him well enough to decipher him somewhat. His countenance was no longer as uncompromising as it had been, but neither was it particularly receptive. *Guarded* was the word that came to mind.

She cleared her throat. Then, unable to bear the thought of, perhaps, reading disbelief in his eyes, she fixed her gaze over his right shoulder and began.

After she'd told him about the money Des owed, Court asked, "How did you get involved with this?"

Heather shrugged. "I did the only thing I could think of to do. I knew the bank wouldn't lend me any more money, so, since Des assured me that there was no way the police could protect him, I went to see Herrera."

Court swore. "Are you crazy?"

Heather smiled slightly. "No, just desperate. I took every cent I had—close to six-hundred dollars, and asked Herrera if he'd agree to some kind of a repayment plan."

"And instead, he came up with this. Placing you here."

Heather shook her head. "No, that was DiMona's plan. He was in Herrera's office." Rising, she moved to the window to stare out at the night. Somewhere out there her brother needed her help.

"What kind of deal did DiMona make with you?"

"I was to come here, spy on you, engage you in conversation, do whatever it took to find out the truth about who and what you were. In exchange they would forget about Des's debt and we could go back to our lives. Only…" Remembering DiMona's face that day, his enjoyment of her pain, she strangled on the words that would voice her fear.

"Only what?"

For a moment, just a moment, doubts assailed her, and Heather hesitated. What if she was wrong about Court? What if, despite everything, he was on the same side as DiMona. What if…? But, there was no help for it. She would have to trust her intuition. Trust Court.

Taking a deep breath, she marshaled her resources. "I don't think he intends to keep his end of the bargain even if I deliver what he wants. Not anymore, if he ever did. I think he means to kill us both. That's why I need your help. I can't save Des by myself." She swallowed. "I might not even be able to save myself."

Court considered her silently. He believed her. Everything he'd learned about her and Des backed up her story.

Did that make him a fool?

Maybe. "You know that DiMona is my associate.

What makes you think that I can protect you, or your brother?''

She studied him in silence for a long moment. ''I don't know,'' she said finally, quietly. ''I just trust you.''

Trust. It was a hard thing to come by. But something told Court, too, that he had to operate on the premise that she was telling the truth. And that meant he had to help her. Somehow. It wouldn't be easy. And he wouldn't be able to do it alone. Which meant convincing his people that she was on the level.

And to do that he needed to know the whole story. ''What did DiMona suspect?''

Heather looked at him. ''You mean why did he want me to spy on you?'' Court nodded, and she continued. ''All he said was that his gut told him there was something not right about you.''

Court considered the implications. As long as DiMona hadn't found anything to confirm his suspicions, everything should still be all right. The Colombians weren't going to sacrifice a useful connection without proof. ''What exactly does DiMona know about me? You've met him a few times now, haven't you? What did you give him?''

Heather shrugged. ''Nothing that satisfied him.'' She detailed the bits and pieces of information she'd passed on. None of it particularly damaging. So Court had that much of an edge at any rate. He immersed himself in his thoughts, considering all the angles, the dangers, the advantages.

A moment later, he looked at her where she stood silhouetted against the night-blackened window of the room, waiting, simply waiting for him to tell her whether he would help her or not. Some women would have continued to talk, to beg, if necessary. But not Heather. She had said her piece, and now she waited. Waited to find out if the man she trusted would help her, or throw her to the wolves.

Her dark-red hair, aflame with the highlights cast by the overhead light, was secured haphazardly on top of her head with a comb. The style revealed the slender curve of her neck. Such a delicate neck. DiMona could have snapped it so easily.

The thought brought Court to his feet? *What had she been thinking to place herself in a position like that?* Ice ran through his veins at the thought of all that could have happened. What could still happen if things went wrong.

Fear for her turned to anger. And that anger needed a focus. With a curse, he drew her attention away from the night. "I can't believe this! What the hell were you thinking to get yourself involved in something like this?"

Her eyes narrowed slightly—an obvious sign of her own rising temper—and he welcomed it. "I was thinking that I had to help my brother. Tell me what I should have done differently, Court."

"You should have gone to the police."

Her eyes flared with sparks. "Oh, sure. And what do you think the police would have said when I told them that my drug-dealing little brother needed help because he'd stolen money from his supplier? Somehow, I don't picture a heck of a lot of sympathy, or help, coming my way."

She had him there. He couldn't predict how the

cops would have reacted. But he couldn't let go of his anger that quickly. "Your brother got himself into the mess, you should have let him get himself out. Take responsibility for his own actions."

"Right. That's what you would have done if you'd had a sister get involved with drugs and get herself into a situation she couldn't see her way out of. You'd have walked away."

Ouch! That barb struck deep. He raked his hair back. "No. No, I guess I wouldn't. But damn it, Heather, wasn't there someone you could have turned to for help?" Before she could answer, he gripped her arms, almost shaking her in his frustration. "Don't you know what could have happened to you?"

She stared up at him, still defiant, still angry. That was his Heather. Never back down. Meet anger with anger. "No!" she all but spat the word. "There was no one I could turn to. Des and I rely on each other. And as for your second question, *yes,* I have a pretty good idea of the kinds of things that could have happened to me. But the day I walk away instead of doing what I can to help someone who needs me, will be the day I can't live with myself anymore."

Her words struck fear into his heart, and this time he did shake her slightly. "And what good is that caring personality going to do anyone if you're dead?"

She gripped his biceps, trying to push out of his grasp. "Stop it! I can't change who I am any more than you can. And you certainly can't change me, so stop trying."

He stared at her. She was right. He couldn't

change her any more than he could change the fact that he was a burned-out cop whose only means of making a living involved standing behind a badge and a gun. A gun that she hated. Yet, despite what his conscious mind might dictate, a deeper more primal impulse told him he had to protect her, not change her. Crushing her to him, holding her tightly enough that not even the DiMonas of the world could take her from him, he said, "You're right. I'm sorry. But, you scare me to death."

Heather closed her eyes. *She* scared *him?* He should try seeing himself from her point of view. "Does that mean you'll help me?" she asked.

"Yes." She felt his lips brush the top of her head. "Yes, I'll help you. Somehow."

Her arms tightened around him and, for the first time in a long time, she reveled in the sensation of leaning on someone else. "Thank you," she murmured.

"You're welcome," he said, the sound little more than a rumble deep in his chest. And then, pulling away from her slightly, he lifted her chin with his finger to look deeply into her eyes for a moment. As though satisfied with what he saw there, he slowly lowered his lips to capture hers. At first the kiss was tender and chaste. But, within an instant, it changed, becoming hungry, needy and so hot.

Desire rose within her with the unstoppable force of an incoming tide. It had been so long…too long. But just as she surrendered to the need within her, she felt him pull away.

"Whoa. I didn't mean for that to happen. I'm sorry."

Swallowing her fear of rejection, of being hurt, of there being no future for two people like them, Heather met his eyes. "I'm not," she said.

As though doubting his own ears, or perhaps her sincerity, Court looked deeply into her eyes. He seemed frozen by indecision. When he still said nothing, Heather reached up to caress his whisker-shadowed cheek. "I need this night, Court. I'm not asking for promises for the future. For once, I just want to live in the moment." She studied his set face. "Please," she added in a near whisper.

A sound, half groan, half growl, erupted from his throat as he drew her into his embrace again. "Don't regret this," he murmured into the shell of her ear.

"I won't," she said just before his lips closed over hers again. Vaguely, she was aware of his hands skimming over her, loosening the tie of her robe, coursing over her naked breasts. His fingers found her turgid nipple, tugged on it gently, and a lightning bolt of sensation rocketed through her, robbing her of strength and breath as it settled, a hot glowing coal, at the juncture of her thighs. Heather clamped her lips to contain the moan of need that rose in her throat, but some small sound must have escaped for Court clasped her to him more tightly.

His hands moved over her shoulders to caress her back, taking the robe with them and, a moment later, it pooled in a heap at her feet. She didn't care.

He tightened his embrace, compressing her full breasts against his chest as he rocked his hips forward, letting her feel the length and breadth of his arousal against her soft belly. And, as molten heat flowed through her veins in answer to Court's unspoken demand for surrender, Heather was thankful that this time there would be no stopping. Whether right or wrong, she needed to find oblivion in his arms. Just for a while.

Wanting nothing more in that instant than to feel his naked flesh against hers, she fumbled with the buttons of his shirt then shoved the garment off of his body. Yes! Yes! Yes! His skin was like satin over steel. Her hands skimmed the silken hair on his chest, moved over the washboard firmness of his abdomen to the zipper on his trousers.

But his hands moved to stay her. "Not yet," he murmured. He stifled her protest by picking her up in his arms and carrying her the few steps to the bed. After laying her down in the center of it, he stood back to look at her, devouring her with his gaze. Her flesh tingled, the nipples of her swollen breasts contracting even more as his gaze raked her from head to toe and back again, hesitating briefly at the triangle of burnished copper curls at the junction of her thighs. "You are so beautiful," he said in a husky tone as his eyes, hard and luminous with arousal, fastened on her face. "You can't imagine how many times I've thought of seeing you like this."

"Probably no more than I have thought of you," she confessed in a murmur. She couldn't help staring at him. Her gaze moved from his hard masculine features that fell just short of handsome to his wide chest and the V of soft dark hair between his pectoral muscles. Over his flat male nipples, down to his muscle-corded abdomen, to his hips where the prominent bulge of his sex was still concealed by his trousers. And then, she lifted her eyes to meet his once more. "Hold me, Court."

It was all the invitation he needed. Bracing his hands on either side of her, he leaned forward to capture her lips, ravaging her mouth and overpowering her senses with his potent masculine assault. Her hands skimmed his body, but once again encountered the frustrating barrier of his trousers. "Your pants," she reminded him when she came up for air. Her fumbling fingers managed to undo them, but as she struggled to push them from his narrow hips, he took over the task.

She had a brief glimpse of his sex jutting from a thick patch of black hair at his groin, and then he was beside her again. So warm, so solid, so strong. Just what she needed to thaw the chill of fear in her soul.

As he covered her face and neck with kisses, his large warm hand closed over her breast, weighing its softness while his thumb caressed the taut nipple. This time she could not contain the groan that escaped her on the heels of the sensation that rocketed through her. Encouraged, his mouth replaced his hand at her breast, closing over the swollen tip, tugging at the tiny crest as he raked the sensitive nub with his tongue. His hand trailed slowly down her body, stopping briefly to delve into her navel before continuing farther to stroke the insides of her thighs. His touch stoked the hot coals of Heather's desire into a raging blaze. Unconsciously seeking to ease the fierce pressure that continued to build, she lifted her hips, pressing herself against the palm of his hand. But it wasn't enough, and she groaned in frustration.

Lifting his head from her breast to look into her face with smoldering eyes, he smiled, a lingering triumphant smile that ignited a fire in her blood. "Now, Court," she demanded.

He shook his head. "You're not ready yet."

Not ready? The man was insane. She was about to explode. "Yes…" she panted. "I am."

Without responding, he rolled over her, nudging her knees apart to kneel between them. She lifted her hips in expectation and invitation, but he merely leaned forward, pressing his sex unsatisfyingly against her as he leaned forward to kiss her. Then, slowly, with torturous precision he trailed a path of fire down her body with his lips and tongue, pausing to torment each of her throbbing nipples to even greater attention before kissing her navel and then tracking even lower. As his mouth closed over that most secret part of her, the last of her control shattered and Heather writhed beneath him. "Now, Court. Please."

And finally, he entered her. Huge and hot and achingly hard, he filled her. She cried out, her hands clutching at the smooth, hard flesh of his back as the tension within her built to a fever pitch. Instinctively, she matched his rhythm, her hips driving upward to meet each of his powerful thrusts until a starburst of perceptions exploded in her brain and waves of sensation impacted, carrying her away on their surging crests. But he gave her no time to linger for he hadn't yet found his release. And before long, his cadential movements had once more stoked the fever in her blood. She clutched at him, seeking anchorage in the storm of desire that raged through her. And this time, when she cried out her satisfaction, he was with her, his hoarse shout echoing hers. Their hearts hammered in unison, and it was a long time before he rolled to one side.

Heather sighed and curled her fingers into the silken hair on his chest, closing her eyes against the slow but inexorable intrusion of reality. It didn't work. And there was one question she had to ask. "Court—"

"Hm?" he responded sleepily.

"Are you—" She swallowed not quite daring to ask.

"Am I what?"

"Are you a cop?"

She sensed his sudden stillness. His hesitation. Lifting her head, she looked up into his face. Into his shuttered eyes. "Trust me?" she murmured. "Please. I need to know that we are trusting each other."

Court studied her expression for a moment. Then, as though reaching a decision, he murmured, "Yeah. I'm one of the good guys." Then, he kissed her brow. "Now, sleep for a little while, sweetheart, and let me do the worrying."

To her surprise, she did.

Chapter 15

Court stared blearily into his coffee. It was 4:12 a.m. according to the digital numerals on his watch. He sighed. Now, when it was almost time to rise, he was finally starting to get tired. He'd hated to leave Heather to wake alone, and he'd wanted nothing more than to hold her throughout the night, but there was too much to do for him to lie in bed when he wasn't able to sleep anyway.

Now that plans had been made and set into motion though, Court found his thoughts returning to Heather. To the way she'd looked, all warm and soft, when he'd slid from her bed. He hoped he got the opportunity to see her that way again. Soon.

Half asleep, he continued to stare dreamily into his coffee. And that's how Ernest found him when he returned to the control room with a fresh pot of coffee. Something in Court's face must have betrayed the direction of his thoughts because Ernest shook his head, then said, ''You know we're going to have to use her to get to DiMona and the kid. There's no other way.''

Everything within Court screamed in protest at the thought of sending Heather into danger, but he only nodded, lifting his tired eyes to meet Ernest's look. ''Yeah, I know.'' His heart gave a painful thud at the admission. How had he come to care for her so much in so short a time?

Ernest appeared about to say something more, but the door of the room opened, surprising them both as Heather entered. ''Hi.'' She wiped her palms against her jean-clad thighs. ''Liz told me where to find you. Mind if I join you?''

''Of course not. Come in.'' Court found her a chair and an awkward silence followed. Looking at her, Court couldn't help but think of the few hours they'd spent together. And how badly he wanted to repeat them.

Meeting his gaze, perhaps reading his mind, color rose in Heather's cheeks. Finally, she cleared her throat, glanced self-consciously at Ernest, and returned her gaze to Court. ''So, what do we do?''

Court sighed inwardly. He didn't want to talk about it anymore, but Heather needed to know. ''The only way we can do anything for your brother is to coordinate his rescue with our other operation. If we move too soon on your brother's behalf, we could tip them off and throw away two years of work and DEA resources. We can thank our lucky stars that the timing is as good as it is.''

Heather frowned slightly. "So how long do we have to wait?"

"It shouldn't be long. We're expecting everything to go down within the next thirty-six to sixty hours."

Heather looked thoughtful, and then slowly nodded. "Okay. The waiting is going to drive me crazy, but...what do you want me to do?"

Court cleared his throat. "We'd prefer to keep you out of it as much as possible—"

"I'm not staying out of it," Heather interrupted him. The vehemence in her voice stunned him. "Des is my brother. Besides you need me to—"

"As I was about to say..." Court interrupted her, in turn. "Unfortunately we can't think of any way around involving you. We need you in order to get to DiMona."

"Oh." Heather flushed. "Sorry."

Court nodded and glanced at Ernest. The two shared a speaking look. *Tell her what she has to do,* Ernest's look said. *Prepare her.* Impatience nipped at Court, but he knew the man was right. They didn't know when the call would come letting them know that it was going down. And when the call came, their superiors might say move *now* or they might say move in six hours. Whatever happened, they had to be ready.

Damn! Every protective instinct within Court balked at what he had to do. Setting aside the fledgling emotion that rose in his throat trying to choke him, refusing to even try to identify it, he sought the words he needed to explain.

"So, then," Heather interrupted his thoughts, "what are you going to want me to do?"

Court looked at her. "The first thing you're going to have to do is set up a meeting with DiMona. The plan is that we'll give you some information to feed him. But, when you meet, you're going to refuse to tell him anything until you see Des. We'll tail you to where he's being held, and then we'll come in and get you."

Heather considered. "It sounds simple enough. But how am I going to know what time to set up the meeting for if you don't know when we can move?"

"Good question. It's one we're still working on. I think what we're going to have to do is wait a while to see if the call comes down. Tonight, if we still haven't heard, then we're going to go ahead and set up the meeting using our best estimate of the timing. We can pretty much guarantee that they'll move at night." And hopefully, somehow in all this mess, he'd get his hands on the proof he needed to put DiMona away. But he couldn't focus on that now. Not with Des Buchanan's life—and possibly Heather's as well—at stake. Even if Court got nothing else on DiMona, he should at least be able to get him on kidnapping.

Five hours later, Heather stood in the breakfast nook sipping hot chocolate as she stared out at another dreary day. *Hold on Des,* she thought, *I'm coming.* At a slight noise from behind, she turned to see Court entering the room. He looked tired, and she noticed that he was limping slightly. "Is your leg bothering you?"

He frowned and shook his head. "Not really. The

strength is fine now. I've noticed, though, that when it's tired it feels like there's a tight elastic band wrapped around my knee."

Heather nodded. "It sounds like the sensation may be starting to come back. It'll take a while, but that's probably a good sign."

He considered her solemnly. "How are you doing?"

She shrugged. "Not bad, I guess. Nervous."

Reaching out, he took the cup from her cold fingers and set it on the table before drawing her into his arms. Wrapping her arms about his waist, she allowed herself to sink into the solace he offered. He was warm and solid and so comforting. His hands moved gently over her back, soothing the tension from the muscles and Heather closed her tired eyes. He just held her for a moment. And then he murmured, "The call came, Heather."

Her eyes flicked open. Then, as the words sank into her tired brain, she reared back to look up into his face. "When?" she demanded.

"Tonight. Ten-thirty. A bit earlier than expected, but for once that works in our favor."

"So you want me to arrange to meet around that time?"

His arms tightened convulsively around her for an instant, and his eyes glowed with some emotion she couldn't recognize as he looked down into her upturned face. Then, he said, "Yeah. About half an hour to an hour before should work. He'll think he has time to meet with you and still be around to supervise his goons when the shipment arrives."

She nodded, and began to move out of his embrace. "I'll make the call."

"Heather—"

"Yes?" She looked back up at him.

But whatever he'd been about to say, the words died on his lips. Finally, he just shook his head and said, "After you make the call, you'd better try to get some sleep. It's going to be a long night."

She forced a smile to her lips. "I will."

Hours later, Heather stood silent while Liz replaced the button on her slacks with another. "This is a transmitter, to help us locate you if something goes wrong. It's not a bug, so we're not going to be able to hear what you're saying. Understand?"

"Yes, but why can't I have one of those? A bug, I mean. Then if something goes wrong I can let you know."

"Wires are too easily detected, and DiMona's not stupid. He'll check you," Court explained. He was leaning against the wall with his arms crossed over his chest looking more rested, but none too happy. "The transmitter is a lower frequency and easy to overlook. If he finds it," he shrugged, "then we're on our own and we'd better not screw up."

Heather swallowed. "I see." For the first time she considered the possibility that, even with Court and the resources of the DEA on her side, she might fail in what she was about to attempt. No! That was unacceptable and she refused to even entertain the potentiality.

Liz stepped back. "Okay. We're about as ready as we can get. Time to go." She left the room, presumably to join Ernest and Dave who were preparing the cars.

Court uncrossed his arms, straightened and moved toward Heather with a loose-limbed confident gait. Only his solemn expression revealed his tension. "I want you to be careful, Heather."

A flicker of irritation passed through her. Why did people insist on stating the obvious? Of course she'd be careful. She wasn't stupid. But before she could open her mouth to say as much, he continued.

"I mean *really* careful. The fact that DiMona has demanded that this meeting take place on a crowded downtown city street means he's wary. He may suspect a setup."

Heather frowned. "I don't know why he should. He's the one that put the forty-eight-hour time limit on getting information."

"All the same, watch him."

She nodded. "Are certain you want me to tell him who you really are?"

Court nodded. "This operation is over anyway, and we want what you tell him to be believable if he checks. I haven't got time to set up anything else. You worry about yourself and Des. Not me. Remember all hell is going to break loose. When it goes down, the first thing you and Des do is hit the floor."

She met his gaze. "I'll—" But, before she had a chance to reassure him, Court swept her into his arms and covered her mouth with his. The kiss was hard, hot, passionate and commanding. And the response it provoked was instantaneous despite where they were, who they were, and what was about to happen. Her breasts swelled. Her heart raced. And a depth charge of excitement exploded in her lower abdomen.

And then, it was over.

"We'll finish this later," Court said as he solemnly brushed a strand of hair back, tucking it behind her ear.

Heather swallowed and managed to find her voice. "Is that a promise?"

His lips stretched into a slow, sexy smile calculated to heat her blood—that gorgeous smile that he used so seldom—and said, "You bet."

And despite all the internal arguments she'd waged against initiating a relationship with this man, with any man who carried a gun and regularly faced danger, Heather hoped he was right. They could deal with the problems facing them later.

The city streets, illuminated by the perpetual twilight of neon lighting and street lamps, hummed with traffic. A fist clenched in Court's gut as he watched DiMona grasp Heather's arm and begin leading her down the crowded street. So far, so good.

Only it didn't *feel* good. Court was more nervous than he had ever been.

A moment later, DiMona handed Heather into a pewter-colored Lincoln and shut the door firmly before walking around the car to get into the driver's seat. Heather's little Volkswagen was being left behind for the second time in as many nights. It had appeared for an instant as though Heather might have argued against abandoning her car, but DiMona had prevailed.

"They're pulling out," Ernest informed him unnecessarily from his position behind the wheel. Although Court was pretty certain that the strength in his leg was now reliable, he didn't want to risk something going wrong tonight, so he'd taken the passenger seat.

He nodded. "Yeah. Get ready."

Ernest put the nondescript sedan they were driving into gear and inched forward. The tail would be conducted by three cars, in constant communication, traveling parallel to each other on different streets. They would switch off every so often, reducing the possibility of being spotted, and they would communicate on a series of predetermined radio channels, making it difficult for anyone to follow their communications. Now, Ernest spoke into the radio. "Suspect on the move. Heading south. We're in pursuit."

The other units confirmed that they'd heard the transmission, and were moving.

After almost an hour of zigging and zagging over half the city of Seattle it seemed, DiMona finally led them to a secluded area of the city where moderately-styled beach houses commanded astronomical prices for their view.

"Isn't this DiMona's own place?" Ernest asked.

Court nodded. "Yeah. I don't like the feel of this." It was out of character for DiMona to let anyone into his personal domain. Court had fully expected to be led to a rented warehouse somewhere. This felt wrong.

He furrowed his brows in thought. Would DiMona have brought the kid here? Possibly. He'd expected to have him for a few days. And he wouldn't have wanted to fall into an easily traceable routine by going somewhere else to take him food. But, if DiMona had brought Des here, why hadn't surveillance seen the kid being brought in? He looked across the car at Ernest. "Is there a way to get to the beachside entrance without being seen?"

Ernest shook his head. "Not unless you arrive by boat."

Boat. Okay, so it was possible the kid could have been brought in without anyone noticing. But, unless the kid had been blindfolded, which was unlikely because something like that would really attract attention in a residential neighborhood like this, it meant that DiMona had never had any intention of letting him go. And, if he was bringing Heather here now, that meant... "Damn!"

"Yup," Ernest agreed, obviously having followed the same lines of thought. "We're gonna have to move in fast."

As DiMona conducted Heather into the beach house kitchen, she anxiously scanned for any sign of Des. The kitchen was empty. In fact, it barely looked lived in. The countertops were bare. No ornaments or dishes sat out. There was only a fridge, a stove and a round oak table with three ladder-back chairs. She met DiMona's cold-eyed look, and carefully keeping all emotion from her voice, asked, "Where is he?"

DiMona's only response was to gesture with a jerk of his head in the direction of an arched doorway that, presumably, led to the living room. Heather moved forward. The instant she was in the

doorway, her eyes found Des. He had been tied to
the missing fourth kitchen chair in the center of the
living room. His mouth had once again been taped
shut with duct tape, and his eyes, wide and frightened, shouted at her to run, to escape. But Heather
couldn't heed his plea. Blind to everything but the
need to touch him, to reassure herself that he was
all right, she began to move toward him only to be
brought up short when DiMona grabbed her arm.

"Okay. You've seen him. Now, what have you
got?"

Heather jerked her arm from his grasp, the fury
she felt on Des's behalf smothering her fear. Meeting DiMona's gaze, it took every ounce of self-
control she possessed not to slap his smug face. Instead, she said the words that could well condemn
them all if Court had miscalculated in the slightest.
"Court Gabriele is a DEA agent." She felt as though
she betrayed Court with those words—even knowing
that she followed the directions he himself had given
her.

DiMona's eyes narrowed. "How do you know?"

"I overheard a conversation he was having with
Ernest. He was telling him that he intended to get
you for the murder of Brett Sanders. He said that
Sanders was his friend and one of the DEA's best
agents and that they had to bring his murderer to
justice."

She met DiMona's gaze squarely, as instructed by
Court. No evasion. For an endless moment, Di-
Mona's soulless eyes seemed to penetrate her soul.
Then, he nodded. "Good. Anything else?"

"No. Now, I want you to release my brother."

DiMona raised a brow. "By all means."

Heather all but raced across the room. Des had sagged in the chair now, and was staring at her with defeated eyes. As her nervous fingers tugged at the tape covering his mouth, she tried to communicate reassurance to him. But he either didn't read her expression, or refused to believe in the promise of hope.

"Oh, Des, are you all right?" she asked him as soon as the tape was clear of his mouth.

"Yeah. Yeah, I'm all right. You shouldn't have come."

Heather began tugging at the ropes binding his hands. She wanted him able to move when the agents stormed the house. "Shouldn't have come! Don't be ridiculous."

Suddenly, a flash and a click drew her attention. Looking over her shoulder, she saw DiMona standing in the center of the room with a camera. At her questioning look, he smiled a mirthless smile. "For posterity," he said.

Des swore. "He takes pictures of the people he kills, Heather."

As Heather's eyes widened in shock, DiMona smirked. "Don't worry if you're not at your best, Heather. It's a private collection." She hated the way he said her name.

As Des's hands came free, he bent to work at the ropes binding his ankles. Heather, thus freed of her task, moved to stand before him facing DiMona.

"Still protecting little brother."

Heather ignored his sarcasm. "You promised me

that if I did what you wanted, we could have our lives back."

He pulled a handgun and a tubelike object from his jacket pocket and began to attach the cylinder to the muzzle of the gun. A silencer! "I lied." He smiled coldly. "You're dead. Both of you."

In the instant before Heather could open her mouth, before DiMona could pull the trigger, the living room window exploded inward in a shower of broken glass. Chaos ensued. Remembering Court's directions to hit the floor, Heather dropped like a stone and dragged Des down with her. And then, all she could do was scrunch her body up into as small a target as possible while shielding her head to try to block out the sounds of violence. She wished for the oblivion of unconsciousness, but her mind refused to comply.

She thought she saw DiMona jerk and clutch his shoulder, but she wasn't sure. He fired his gun in a continuous volley in the direction of the window.

Bullets whined. Men shouted. Someone screamed in pain and swore. Another voice yelled, "He's getting away. Son of a bitch! Where the hell did he go?"

Oh, no! Where was DiMona? Still here somewhere? Would he try to carry out his threat before he was caught?

Where was Court? Was he all right?

Chapter 16

Someone swore again. "Okay. I want a thorough search of this place. No stone left unturned."

Heather held her breath. *Please catch him.* DiMona's threat resounded in her mind. She didn't want to die.

A hand fell on her shoulder, and she jumped, a muffled squeal of terror escaping her throat before she could contain it. "Whoa, there. It's Court. Are you okay?"

At the sound of his familiar voice, the terror faded somewhat and she sat up, nodding jerkily in response to his question. "Yes." Relief poured through her that he, too, appeared unhurt. "Des?"

"Right here, Sis." He was sitting just behind and to her right. Now, he got to his feet and moved forward, his gaze on Court as though he sensed the undercurrents between this stranger and his sister, and was trying to interpret them. He looked at her. "Is this the client?"

Heather nodded as she accepted Court's silently offered hand to get to her feet. Des had always been very intuitive. "This is Court Gabriele. Or rather, Court Morgan." Court had told her his real name when he'd been briefing her on what to tell DiMona. But it was difficult to suddenly start thinking of him as another person. "He's with the DEA."

Des nodded and offered his hand to Court. "I'm Des Buchanan." Despite the ordeal he'd been through, Des seemed different in some way—more self-assured—but Heather didn't have the opportunity to pay much heed to the passing observation.

As Court accepted Des's hand, the two men sized each other up. Des obviously decided to get worry out of the way first. "Am I under arrest?"

Court considered him. "Not at the moment. But, I daresay you'll have a lot of explaining to do before this is over."

Des nodded. "Understood." His gaze shifted to the chaos surrounding them. "Did you get him?"

Court met his gaze silently for a moment, briefly turned his head to meet Heather's worried look, then shook his head. "No. He got out on the beachside of the house. Took off in a boat. But we'll get him. We've got him on kidnapping and unlawful confinement now, and we're looking for more evidence."

"Do you know about the pictures?" Heather asked.

Court frowned. "We found a camera. An expensive digital model."

Des shook his head. "That's not what she means.

DiMona saved pictures.'' He went on to explain how DiMona had taunted him with the idea of increasing his collection.

Court nodded. ''We'll look for them.'' Someone yelled his name, and he looked over his shoulder.

''We've got keys,'' the voice said. Heather thought it sounded like Ernest. ''One that looks like it could be for a safety deposit box.''

''Great!'' Court yelled in response before turning his attention back to Heather. ''We'll be finished here in a little while. It would probably be best if you waited in the car.''

''No!'' Realizing that her tone was almost frantic, Heather modulated her tone. ''What if DiMona comes back and we're out there while all of you are in here?'' She shook her head. ''He said he was going to kill us.''

Court considered her. At first glance, she seemed remarkably composed considering the harrowing time she'd been through. But a closer look revealed that her composure was brittle. Heather was strong— life had made her that way—but even she had limits. Ignoring the expression on young Des Buchanan's face, Court put his arms around her. ''I won't let him get to you, Heather,'' he murmured into her ear. ''You have my word on that. All right?''

He heard her draw a shaky breath, and then she nodded. He rubbed her back for a moment, and felt some of the tension begin to ease from her body. ''You and Des just wait over there for me then.'' He indicated a spot against one wall that didn't appear as though it would be of any interest to those doing the evidence collection. ''I'll be with you as soon as I can." And somehow, between now and then, he had to come up with a way to keep his promise, to keep her safe.

Damn! He was digging himself deeper and deeper into a hole that he wasn't sure he could find his way out of without losing part of himself. Any relationship between them was hopeless. They were simply too far apart. He didn't know how to be anything other than what he was. And she wouldn't live her life with a man who represented something she hated. So why the hell didn't he pass the responsibility for her protection on to someone else and save himself the headache?

Damned if he knew the answer to that question.

Turning back to the room and his job, he walked over to Dave. The young agent had taken a bullet in the shoulder during the initial moments of the strike, but it was a clean wound. "How you doin'?"

Despite the pain written on his face, Dave tried to smile. "I'll live."

Court nodded. "The ambulance should be here any minute. Just take it easy, okay?"

Dave nodded. "Yeah. It's not quite the way I pictured it, you know. I feel like I should be telling you it's just a flesh wound—like in the movies—but it's not like that."

Court's mouth twisted in a wry smile as he squeezed Dave's uninjured shoulder. "It never is, man. It never is."

The sun was coming up when Court ushered Heather and Des onto the small twin-engine airplane he'd chartered. They were all exhausted, but all in all—from a professional point of view—it hadn't been a bad night. Doug Grey, his legal partner, had earned immunity from the prosecution for his complete cooperation with the DEA. Channing had lost everything his illicit profits had purchased, but he'd earned a reduced sentence for his help. The Seattle cell of the cartel had been dealt a mortal blow while still in its infancy. The Agency had a total of three injured agents, but they had made over thirty high-profile arrests including Aponte and Antonio Vargas.

From a personal standpoint, another hit had been dealt to the people who had been responsible for his sister, Carly's, death. And Court thought maybe, just maybe, this time it would be enough for him to find peace. He was getting too old for this work. Or at least he felt like he was, which amounted to the same thing.

The only major player who had escaped the net was Rick DiMona. This time, though, they had enough evidence to issue a warrant. And, once they found those pictures, enough evidence to put him away for a long, long time when they did catch up with him. Enough evidence to ensure that Brett Sanders's murderer would finally pay.

It was pure poetic justice that DiMona's own actions in sending Heather into Court's home and then kidnapping Des had finally allowed the DEA and Court to find the evidence that they would not otherwise have found.

As Court sat beside Heather in the small eight-seater aircraft, he gripped her fingers and squeezed reassuringly. "Where are we going?" she asked in a tired voice.

"I promised you I'd keep you and Des safe." He glanced toward the young man across the narrow aisle who gave the appearance of having fallen asleep the moment he'd taken his seat. "So I'm taking you home."

"Your *real* home?"

He nodded. "Yeah."

"Where is it?"

Court allowed a weary smile to touch his lips. "A ranch in Montana. It'll be a hell of a lot harder for anyone to get close to us there without being seen."

Heather considered the idea. There were probably a million questions she should ask, and would have asked if her tired brain would function. "That sounds…good."

"Yeah. Sleep for a while if you can."

To her surprise, she could. And did.

Heather must have been dead tired because she didn't even wake when the small plane landed. It took Court shaking her shoulder and calling her name to rouse her. Blinking against the fog of sleep that still clouded her eyes, she looked around. Across the narrow aisle, Des still slept as well. "Are we there?"

"This is the airstrip at Big Springs," Court replied. "My brother will be here to take us to the ranch."

Heather blinked up at him. "Your brother? But… Oh, of course." All the information Court had given her had been false. The details associated with the fictional persona of Court Gabriele, not Court Morgan. It was going to take some getting used to. "So, do you have any other family I should be aware of?"

Court nodded. "My mother, Kate. She's widowed. Dad's been dead about ten years now, so we'll be staying with her. She'd never admit it, but she loves the company. And then there's, my sister, MacKenzie. Kenzie lives here in town."

"Kenzie? That's an unusual nickname."

Court shrugged. "It's what Chase called her when we were little, and it stuck."

"Chase is your brother?"

"Yup." Court looked out the window of the taxiing plane. "There he is now."

Heather followed his gaze to see a tall man dressed in jeans, a blue denim shirt and a black cowboy hat standing next to a dark-green sport utility vehicle parked on the tarmac. She was trying to determine if he looked anything like Court, but, just when they were getting close enough to discern details, the plane turned, and she lost sight of him. Five minutes later though, as she and Des sat in the back of the Land Rover on the way to the ranch while Court and Chase sat in the front catching up, it was easy to see that the brothers looked very much alike except in the way they dressed.

They shared the same features, the same thick black hair and the same proud carriage. The most obvious difference that Heather could see was in their eyes. Chase's eyes, were a unique blue-grey color that reminded Heather of nothing so much as a summer thundercloud.

Des looked out at the passing countryside. "It's nice here," he commented.

Heather nodded. Green fields and hills rolled toward blue-tinged mountains in the distance. "Yes," she said. "It is."

"Look. There's a porcupine." Des pointed at a spiny creature waddling along at the side of the gravel road.

She smiled, and then as Des fell silent again, content to simply look around, she eavesdropped unashamedly on the conversation taking place in the front seat.

"Does Mom know you're coming?" Chase asked.

Court nodded. "Yeah. I called."

"What about Kenzie?"

"No, I didn't get a chance to call her. I suppose I'd better, huh?"

Chase eyed his brother. "I'd say so. If she finds out you came home and didn't even call I wouldn't lay odds on her ever speakin' to you again." He dug in his shirt pocket and pulled out a small cellular phone. "Here."

Court had no sooner concluded his conversation with his sister than Chase slowed the Land Rover to turn into a drive over which an enormous carved wooden sign that read Rocking-M Ranch had been raised. The drive, bordered on both sides by huge elms that arched over it, led to a low, rambling ranch-style house. An enormous covered veranda, ablaze with potted flowers, stretched across the entire front of the structure. As the Land Rover came to a sudden halt in the gravel drive, the front door opened and a woman who appeared to be in her sixties stepped out. She had snow-white hair, but she was slim and vital with a stride as steady and firm as any woman half her age. Wearing jeans, a chambray work shirt and cowboy boots, there was something about the woman that reminded Heather of Barbara Stanwyck in the old *Big Valley* reruns.

"Chase Morgan," the woman shouted, "if I've told you once, I've told you a thousand times, *slow down.* One of these times your gonna come drivin' straight into my livin' room."

"Yes, ma'am," Chase returned as Court got out of the vehicle and opened the rear door for Heather. Des was already sliding out the other side.

Gripping Heather's elbow, Court led her and Des up the veranda steps. "Mom, I'd like to introduce my friends, Heather and Des Buchanan. My mother, Kate Morgan." As hands were shaken all around, Kate studied both Heather and Des with an astute steel-hued gaze that seemed to miss nothing. Finally she nodded slightly and smiled. "Welcome," she said simply. "Come in."

The screen door squealed slightly on its hinges as she opened it, and they stepped into the house. Following Kate's lead, rather than removing her shoes, Heather simply wiped them thoroughly on the mat at the door. Des, she noted, followed suit as did both Court and Chase. She guessed that on a working ranch it was probably too much trouble to be pulling cowboy boots on and off.

The house was shady and cool. Its interior was filled with old but well cared for furniture and the knicknacks provided by a lifetime of living. There were children's handprints set in plaster hanging on the wall along with myriad photos of people and animals. A shot of a prize-winning bull graced the wall right next to a school picture of a young girl. Kenzie, Heather assumed. Perhaps the bull had been hers.

And then they were in the kitchen. A very large kitchen. The country-pine table would easily seat eight people. "How long's it been since you ate?" Kate asked. "Did you have any breakfast?"

"No, ma'am," Court responded. "We left in a bit of a hurry."

She nodded. "Well, sit yourselves down then, and I'll fix something." She looked at her younger son. "What about you, Chase?"

"No, thanks, Mom. I ate, but I wouldn't mind some of your coffee."

She nodded. "Help yourself then," she said as she removed a stack of bacon wrapped in brown freezer paper from the refrigerator. "It's a fresh pot."

She looked at Des. "Bacon and eggs okay with you city folks?" she asked with a grin on her face.

"Yes, ma'am," Des responded. Heather looked at him in surprise. It was the first time she'd ever heard him call anyone *ma'am*. But then she supposed there was something about Kate Morgan with her gruff but caring manner that simply demanded that kind of respect.

When Heather switched her gaze back to Kate, she realized the woman was still waiting for her response. "Bacon and eggs are fine. Thank you."

Heather stared out the window of the room she'd been given at the night sky. A full moon hung low in the horizon bathing the rolling hills of the ranch in silver. The night was filled with noise, but the sounds, so different from those heard in the city, emphasized the solitude. Rather than the humming of tires on pavement, she listened to the croaking of frogs and the singing of crickets. The honking of car horns had been replaced by the excited yipping and howling of coyotes in pursuit of prey. The sounds of human voices talking, shouting, laughing had been supplanted by the quiet quacking of ducks on the pond. Sighing wistfully, Heather leaned her head against the cool glass of the window. It was so beautiful here. So peaceful. She wished...

If wishes were horses, my girl, then beggars would ride. Moira Buchanan's voice played in her daughter's mind. Oh, how Heather missed her. Missed having a family. She hadn't realized how much until today when she and Des had been enfolded into the Morgan family as though it was where they belonged. It had been so long since she'd been part of a family that consisted of more than two people, and it felt good.

Her mind turned to Court, to they way he'd gradually relaxed throughout the day. Teased mercilessly by his brother and sister. Pestered incessantly by his mute young nephew, Danny, who constantly placed toys in his uncle's hands. Danny was Chase's son, she had learned. The child had been just learning to speak when his mother was murdered. It was believed that Danny had witnessed the murder, for he had never spoken since. Her heart ached for the little boy, but it ached more for the man she was growing to love.

Did she dare dream of the possibility that she and Court might have something lasting between them?

No, it was probably better to live for the moment. It would hurt when the time came to part, but... She'd have to be blind not to see that the entire focus of Court's life was his work. There seemed to be little room in his life for a woman. Certainly no room for the possibility of love. And despite herself, despite everything that had happened in her life, Heather still dreamed of a traditional marriage forged with love...and a man who came home every night.

Suddenly, her attention was caught by the sight of a familiar figure in the yard below. Des. What was he doing up? She observed him a moment, but all he did was walk to the fence where he stood looking at the sky. Since they hadn't had much chance to talk in the last while, she decided to take this opportunity to slip down and speak to him.

He heard her approach as her feet crunched on the gravel and turned to greet her. "Hi, Sis. How you doing?"

"All right. Mind if I join you?"

He shook his head. "Naw. I was just enjoying the night. I know we've only been here a few hours, but... Well, there's something about it. It's beautiful here, isn't it?"

Heather nodded. "It sure is." They stood side by side in silence for a time and then Heather broached a topic that had been on her mind. "You seem different, Des."

"How so?" He glanced at her.

Heather shrugged, trying to put into words the nebulous quality that no one but she, who knew him so well, would have noticed. "I don't know. You seem more…not happier exactly, but *content,* I guess. Does that make sense?"

He nodded. "Yeah, it does."

"So, what happened to affect this change?"

"When I was in the rehab center, Dr. Ward figured out what was wrong with me. I have clinical depression, Sis. A treatable illness."

Heather stared at him, unable to comment.

"How—how did Dr. Ward arrive at that conclusion?" she asked finally.

"My symptoms," Des said. "The lack of concentration, the mood swings and periodic depression, the poor judgment, the tendency toward addiction. Add to that Dad's descent into depression when Mom died and his suicide, and Dr. Ward came to the conclusion that I may have inherited a familial tendency toward depression which was triggered by witnessing the shooting."

That's how Des had always referred to it: *the shooting.* "Do you remember it now?" Heather asked.

Des shook his head. "No. According to Dr. Ward I buried the memory so deep it may never surface, which is fine. He doesn't think I need to remember the details in order to put it behind me and move on."

Heather swallowed. "So, Dr. Ward has given you medication? An anti-depressant?"

Des nodded and removed a small flat pillbox from his shirt pocket. "One every morning. It's as simple as that."

"I'm surprised that DiMona let you keep the pills."

Des shrugged. "I hid them in my socks before going to see him. He never checked my ankles."

Heather put her arm around him. "I'm glad you found what you needed, Des. All I've ever wanted for you is that you be happy." Now, if only she could find happiness…. Her thoughts returned to Court and the seemingly insurmountable obstacles that faced them.

Chapter 17

"You can't go back with me, Heather," Court said. His voice was cool and controlled, but threaded with steel. "It's out of the question. The reason I brought you here was so that you'd be safe while I tracked down DiMona."

It was late morning on their second day on the ranch. Court had just informed her that he had to be back at work in Seattle the next evening. And Heather intended to go with him whether he liked it or not. "It's me he wants, not you," she reminded him. "How do you know he'll even surface if I'm not with you?"

"I don't. But if he doesn't, we'll find another way to get him. I refuse to put you at risk again."

Heather stared at him, seeking a more convincing argument. It was difficult to explain, even to herself, the feeling she had that told her she must return. It was as though, by facing DiMona, she could seize back the control that had been lacking in her life for so long. DiMona had terrorized her, and in so doing had, in some way, come to represent all the fears she'd lived with for the last ten years. To conquer that fear, instinct told her she needed to face him again. Not hide and wait in fear for him to come to her. She needed to face him and win—if she could. She needed to finish it for herself, to achieve a sense of closure. But how to convince Court of that?

"It should be my decision, not yours," she argued.

"Wrong! Jeez, I've never met a more stubborn woman."

Heather stared at him indignantly. "If you think calling me stubborn and treating me like a child incapable of making my own decisions is going to convince me that you're right, then you're sadly mistaken."

Court closed his eyes and took a deep breath before responding. "You're right. I apologize." He crossed the room to take her in his arms. "Heather, please try to understand. I can't do my job properly if I'm worried sick about you. And, not being able to do my job properly could be dangerous."

She didn't want to be responsible for him getting hurt. Neither, though, did she want to stay safely ensconced on the ranch while he went off to slay her dragon. She needed to see with her own eyes that the dragon was gone or she'd never be at peace. Why was he being so obstinate? "You'll have a better chance of catching him if you have the bait he wants, Court."

"I can't use you as bait. Don't you understand that, Heather?"

She looked into Court's amber eyes, trying to read the emotions written there, but it was useless. Did Court care about her more than he'd let on? Was that perhaps why he felt that he needed to protect her so carefully? But that was a question she could never ask, for she was afraid of the answer. "I think so," she allowed. But that didn't mean she could abide by his wishes.

"Good. Then let's not argue about it anymore. I'd like to enjoy the time we have together." Before she could respond, Court swept her into his arms and gave her one of his soul-shattering kisses. Then, while her senses were still befuddled, he said, "Come on. Let's have a picnic. We'll saddle a couple of horses and get away—just the two of us. Okay?"

Heather struggled to think. She didn't want to ruin the time she and Court had left together with arguments either. But... "What about Des?"

"He's gone off with Kenzie to look at computer stuff. Those two are kindred spirits. Kenzie was even talking about hiring him to help her out occasionally, and she never lets anyone into her office."

"Oh." Well, she guessed that settled the one and only argument she had against going. Not that she really wanted one. She smiled. "A picnic sounds wonderful."

Two hours later, Court reigned his big bay gelding, Benny, to a halt in a high meadow and waited for Heather's dainty sorrel mare to pick her way toward him. "How about over there?" he suggested, indicating a shady spot just a little above the stream that flowed off to their right. "We'll leave the horses to graze by the stream." The spot he'd indicated was blanketed with wildflowers and bordered by a rocky hillside and the stream.

Heather smiled. "It looks perfect."

Dismounting, they led the horses to the stream. Court instructed Heather on how to ground-tether her mount by simply allowing the reigns to dangle. Then, they unloaded their blanket and picnic supplies.

Sometime later, replete and content, Heather lay on her back on the blanket, staring up at the brilliant-blue sky through the boughs of a spruce tree while Court held a small buttercup flower beneath her chin trying to determine whether she liked butter or not. "Yup," he concluded. "I'd say you *love* butter."

Heather laughed. "That I do." He began to trace the flower gently over her chin and cheeks and Heather couldn't help wondering what could ever have prompted him to leave this place. "What made you become a cop?"

His gaze lifted to meet hers, and the teasing light slowly faded from their depths. Heather realized that in some way she'd trod on something private. To reassure him, she lifted her hand to cup his whisker-shadowed cheek. "It's all right. You don't have to tell me."

He shook his head. "No, it's okay. Really. You just caught me by surprise." He rolled over onto his back and stared up into the sky. For the longest time, he remained silent. Then, finally, he spoke. "I had an older sister named Carly. We were only a year apart, and about as close as a brother and sister can get. But Carly had a wild streak a mile wide, and she quit school right after high school to take off for the big city. She ended up in Los Angeles, angry and rebellious and determined to prove that she needed no one." He fell silent a moment, then drew an audible breath before speaking again. "Within a year she was dead."

Heather gasped at the brutal finality in the way he spoke the words. "What happened?"

He shrugged. "She met the wrong kind of people. They got her into drugs. By the time she admitted to herself that she needed help and called home to let us know where she was, it was too late. Dad and I got there to take her home, but she was already dead of an overdose."

"Oh, I'm so sorry, Court."

He nodded. "Yeah. It was rough. I blamed myself. I was closer to her than anyone else. Maybe if I'd tried a little harder, I could have found her sooner. Could have gotten her to come home. But, I was angry with her for leaving, so I didn't. And after she was gone, there was no way to make it up to her. I decided there was only one way to give her death meaning—I had to find and punish the people who were responsible for her death."

He fell silent, and Heather concluded for him. "So you became a cop."

"Yeah. I figured joining the DEA would be the best way, so I set out with that in mind. It took a while, but I made it."

"And did you ever find the people responsible for Carly's death?"

"No." He shrugged slightly. "But I like to think that I may have gotten them anyway by just doing my job. It's taken a lot of years, but I don't feel quite so guilty any more."

Heather sighed and rose on her elbow to look down into Court's face. "I know about guilt."

"I know you do," he murmured as he lifted his hand to brush her hair behind her ear. "We're a lot alike, you and I." Then, cupping the nape of her neck, he tugged her down to kiss her.

Yes, they were. And that made her wonder...

She was falling in love with him, but afraid to face that fact and all the choices that would come with it. And, now, hope—foolish hope—began to blossom in her heart that maybe, just maybe, he, too, was growing to love her.

Rick DiMona lowered the binoculars and smiled a self-satisfied smile as he gripped the case that carried his high-powered rifle, pulling it closer. Years of practice enabled him to assemble the weapon in mere minutes. He made a minor adjustment to the telescopic sight, attached the silencer that would muffle the report, and then settled down to await the perfect shot.

Damn, he was good! Armed with little more information than Brett Sanders's name, he had used every avenue of information available to him, and he had found Court Gabriele. Or rather, Court Morgan. It hadn't been as difficult as he'd anticipated, actually. Simply a matter of determining who had been Brett Sanders's closest friends within the agency. Who would have taken his murder personally.

Court Morgan's name had come up readily enough. And then Rick had simply had to pay enough high-priced computer gurus to track down everything they could. Within six hours, one of them had provided DiMona with the location of the Rocking M Ranch. Since he knew Morgan would have taken the bitch and her brother to somewhere secluded, he gambled on this being the place.

The gamble had paid off.

Rick had staked the ranch out. Watching. Waiting. Anticipating the opportunity of catching Heather Buchanan and Court in the open. He wanted them both so badly he could taste the bitter tang in his mouth. The hate, the need to kill them for what they'd done, was like a fever in his blood.

Court Gabriele and his associates had circumvented Rick's security measures, tumbling the empire he'd been building. Hypocritical cops had stolen his life once. He wouldn't allow them to get away with it again.

And Heather…Heather had dared to defy him. To betray him. To screw up his plans. It was partially because of her that he'd lost this round. And he never accepted defeat. Only by killing her could he transform his defeat into a draw. Although he still wouldn't like it, *that* he could accept.

Win was his only motto. The cost of the win was unimportant.

Now, he watched the lovers for a time, awaiting the perfect moment. Their laughter drifted to him on the heels of a crisp breeze, and he allowed the sound to fan the ice-cold flames of his hatred. He'd take out the cop first, he decided. Get him out of the way. Then he could deal with the woman at his leisure.

"We need to find a more private spot." Court observed as he looked down into Heather's flushed face.

"Why?" she asked.

He chucked her under the chin. "Do you really need to ask?"

She grinned. "No, I guess not." Then she glanced beyond him. "But if we don't catch those horses soon, we won't be going anywhere."

Court looked over his shoulder. "They won't go far. They're just grazing." Even as he watched them though, both horses' heads came up sharply and they looked back the way they'd come.

Had somebody followed them?

"What?" Heather began to speak.

As a sudden chill raised the hair on the back of his neck, Court placed a finger over Heather's lips to halt her words. "Shh." Without moving enough to draw attention to himself if he hadn't yet been noticed, he scanned the surrounding hills. Was that a flash of light on glass?

Instinct told him there was a threat out there somewhere. From who or what, he didn't know. Damn! He should have chosen a spot that provided more shelter. There was a single large boulder about fifteen feet away, but that was it. And the horses were a good thirty yards away across on open grassy meadow.

"Come on," he said, rising to his feet in one fluid motion as he held out a hand to Heather. "We're leav—" But in the next instant something kicked his leg out from under him with tremendous force, and he collapsed in an ungainly heap. "What the—"

"Oh, my God! You're bleeding!" Heather's voice was frantic as she dropped to her knees at his side.

He looked down at his right leg to see a small geyser of blood squirting from a wound high on his thigh before Heather placed her hand over the injury, putting pressure on the wound. "It's not bad," she assured him quickly. "Just a slight nick to the artery, I think."

He'd been shot!

In the next instant, he was moving. "Get behind the boulder," he yelled, trying to push Heather to safety.

Not bothering to waste her breath on argument, Heather gave him a furious look that told him more clearly than words just what she thought of his plan. Then, scooting around behind him, she gripped him beneath the arms and began dragging him toward the boulder.

"Damn it, woman! Will you never listen?" he asked as he pushed with his good leg, helping her to maneuver his body across the ground.

"Only when you make sense," she gasped out as she strained to drag him while keeping them both low to the ground. Smaller targets.

Something that sounded like a bee whistled by Heather's ear, struck the boulder toward which they were moving and whined off in an unknown direction. Heather muttered an uncharacteristic curse beneath her breath. She was terrified. For both of them, but more for Court.

She needed to slow the bleeding and get him help as quickly as possible, or he could bleed to death. The thought of losing him… She refused to contemplate it.

Apparently realizing that she wasn't about to leave him, no matter the danger, Court shoved harder, helping her to get them both behind the huge boulder. Two more near-miss shots whistled by them, but they made it.

Propelled by icy fear, as soon as they'd reached the relative security the large stone provided, Heather removed Court's shirt and, using teeth, hands and finally Court's jackknife on the sturdy fabric, managed to tear it into strips. Moving as quickly as was humanly possible, she bound the wound as tightly as she could without cutting off the blood supply. Then, she used a doubled strip of cloth to fashion a tourniquet through which she inserted a small but thick branch that Court could use to tighten and loosen the tourniquet as needed. That done, she finally slowed the frantic pace at which she'd been moving and sat back on her heels to meet Court's eyes. "How is it?"

He shrugged. "Deep down, where it should hurt, I can't feel a thing. But I've got one of those pain echo things happening on the surface. Hurts like hell."

Heather nodded. "We need to get you to a doctor." She looked around as though the answer to her dilemma would surface in their surroundings, then looked back at Court. "Any ideas?"

Grimacing against his pain, he stared thoughtfully at the horses. Although they twitched and stamped nervously, both well-trained horses had stayed pretty much where they were. "There's a cell phone in Benny's saddlebags, but that might not be any help anyway. The reception up here isn't always the greatest. The rifle is on the horse, and there's no way to get to the horses." He was talking aloud, almost musingly as he tried to plan their way out. "All we've got is…" He leaned forward and tugged the hem of his jeans up until his boot was exposed. Then, with a grunt of satisfaction, he removed a small handgun from his boot top. "…this," he concluded wearily.

Heather nodded as she took the small gun from his hand to study it. "A .38?" she asked for verification.

He looked at her in surprise. "Yeah. It's a .38 Chief's Special." He grimaced at a sudden pain, and then commented, "I thought you hated guns."

She met his gaze. "I do. But you have to know something before you can hate it. My counsellor always said, 'It's best to know your enemy.' He advised me to take shooting lessons and get to know guns in order to get over my fear of them."

Court eyed her curiously. "It didn't work?"

Heather shrugged. "Oh, it worked, I guess. As long as the gun is in *my* hand."

She paused, looking at him worriedly. "What do we do?"

Court's expression was grim as he looked back toward the rocks from where the shots had come. Then he met Heather's eyes. "I'm in rough shape, sweetheart. So, I'm going to have to rely on you to get us out of this. Okay?''

Heather swallowed. She didn't want the responsibility, but there was no other way. Not with Court so badly injured. Nodding, she asked, ''What do I have to do?''

''Since we can't get to the horses, you're going to have to work your way around the other way, using the rocks on the hill as cover. You'll have to get behind the shooter and…'' He gasped in sudden pain. ''And disarm him, or take him out, or something. Whatever works. A handgun against a sniper's rifle makes the odds a bit uneven, but its all we've got. I'll do my best to keep his attention focused on me while you get close to him.''

Heather eyed the path he'd outlined. Some of the rocks looked barely large enough to conceal her. But that wasn't what was bothering her. ''Court…I don't think I can kill a man.''

Court considered her. ''I wouldn't ask you to kill anyone, Heather. Just try to get the drop on him. Make him give up his weapon. If it comes down to it, and you have to shoot, aim for his leg or another nonvital part. Understood?''

Slowly, Heather nodded. ''Understood.'' But could she do it?

''Good. Once you've disarmed him, you're going to find yourself in a standoff situation. If you get too close to him, he could overpower you and take the gun. So, keep your distance.''

Heather nodded. She could see his reasoning, but… As though sensing the direction of her thoughts, Court continued. ''That's where I come in,'' he said. ''Once you've gained control up there so that I can get into the open without getting shot, I'll grab Benny and come up to help.''

Heather took a deep breath. ''Okay.'' The plan was the best they were going to get, so she'd better make it work. ''I guess that means I'd better leave you with some means of maneuvering. A crutch or something.''

He nodded. ''Good point.''

She spotted a large stout branch nearby that, if it wasn't too old and brittle, would suffice. Although it certainly wouldn't be comfortable for Court. With a cautious glance over her shoulder to gauge whether or not she'd be exposing herself, she crept forward to grab it.

Darn! At close range she realized it was too short.

Sensing her hesitation, Court said, ''It will work as a cane, Heather, and we're not about to find anything better.''

Realizing he was right, Heather grabbed the branch and crept back to his side. Then she swallowed, facing the question she'd avoided until this point. ''Who do you think is up there?''

Court considered her solemnly as he automatically tightened the tourniquet again. ''DiMona,'' he said finally. ''Its got to be DiMona.''

Heather nodded. ''That's what I figure, too.'' The decision of who would face DiMona, and when, had been taken out of their hands. Heather had to face him alone and triumph quickly enough to get help for Court. Court had saved her life—hers and Des's—by storming DiMona's beach house and now it was her turn to repay him.

If she could. She wondered what odds a Las Vegas bookie would offer for her chances of success. The possibility of failure made her realize that there was something she had to say to Court before she left. Because she might not ever have another chance.

Reaching out, she laid her hand against Court's whisker-roughened cheek. "Court. This isn't the best time to say this, and I may be making a complete fool of myself, but I want you to know before I... Well, just in case things don't..."

Court looked at her with worry-shadowed eyes. "What is it, baby?"

"I—I love you." She blurted the words out before second thoughts could make her hold her tongue. Then, coward that she was, without waiting for a response, without even waiting to see Court's reaction, she scurried over to the next boulder.

"Heather—" Court called after her in a stage whisper, but she ignored him. The last thing she wanted was to hear him try to let her down easy. She knew as well as he did that there was little hope of them sharing a life together. He was a career cop, married to his job, and she doubted that there was room in his life for him to love anything or anyone else. And she simply couldn't bear the uncertainty of being married to someone who faced danger every day. Unfortunately, that hadn't prevented her from falling in love with him, but there was little she could do about that now.

"Damn it, woman, you can't say something like that and then just take off. I have something to tell you, too."

Heather looked back at him. "Tell me later," she whispered. She took a deep breath and focused on the jumble of rocks where DiMona had concealed himself. It was now or never, and failure was not an option.

Chapter 18

Ignoring her trembling hands, Heather focused on climbing toward the spot where Court believed DiMona had concealed himself. She was terrified, but she didn't have any choice. Even if she and Court could have gotten to the horses, with DiMona still up there with a rifle, they wouldn't have stood a snowball's chance in hell of riding out of the meadow alive.

Inside the waistband of her jeans, she felt the small handgun pressing against her back. A constant reminder of what might be required of her when she reached DiMona. Could she do it if she had to?

A vision of Court bleeding to death in the shelter of the boulder while waiting for help flashed in her mind. She wouldn't allow that to happen. She couldn't! She'd face a lifetime of counseling to deal with that trauma. So, she'd do what she had to do to get them out of there. That was all there was to it.

Her resolve solidified, Heather crept to the next boulder. And the next. She heard the pop of another shot, followed by a ricochet and knew that Court had done something to keep DiMona's attention on him. *Please, God, keep him safe,* she prayed. She was almost there.

Catching sight of DiMona's head in the rocks just above and to her right, she ducked. Court had said she had to get behind him, surprise him.

Stepping cautiously to avoid loose stones, she continued on, seeking a way to do as Court had directed. There! A place to move into the rocks behind him. She'd come out a little above him, but...

She was about fifteen feet behind him now, on a ledge only about four feet above the large flat area DiMona had chosen to shoot from. But getting down to that area wouldn't be easy. There was no path, and the sloped area between the two ledges was covered with loose shale which would alert DiMona to her presence if she attempted to walk down. She couldn't jump without climbing up onto the boulder behind which she was concealed, which meant adding another three or four feet to the distance. And a jump of seven feet would definitely make enough noise to attract DiMona before she could regain her footing. She'd have to distract him first.

Picking up a fist-size stone, she was about to throw it off to the left, when a small shower of gravel fell from her ledge, and she froze in horror. DiMona spun, bringing his rifle to bear on her almost before his gaze found her—which happened so

quickly she didn't even have the chance to duck.
Then, he grinned. "Well, well, well. What have we
here?" He answered his own question. "Just what I
was wishin' for. A hostage." The smile faded from
his lips as though it had never been, and he eyed the
stone in her hand. "Don't tell me you were going
to hit me over the head." He didn't wait for her
response. "That's not very friendly, Heather."
Something in his eyes grew colder. "Get your ass
down here before I decide to shoot you where you
stand."

Heather's mind raced. She didn't want to comply,
but she didn't know what to do. She'd screwed up.
Royally. "Okay. Okay. I'm coming," she assured
him, automatically raising her hands.

The instant she reached the lower ledge, DiMona
grabbed her arm, directed her to toss the stone
away—which she did, reluctantly—and dragged her
over to the position he'd occupied overlooking the
meadow below.

For an instant, Heather stared at him in shock. He
hadn't searched her! He didn't know she was armed!
And with the gun firmly concealed by the tail of her
blouse and the waistband of her jeans, he wouldn't
know until… Heather flicked a glance skyward.
*Thank you, God. Now if you could just spare a little
guidance…*

"Hey, cop," DiMona yelled abruptly, startling
Heather. "I've got your girlfriend. Come on out and
maybe we'll talk."

"What are you doing?" Heather demanded.
"You shot him. How can he possibly come out?"

She hoped to convince DiMona that Court was either dead or too far gone to be a threat. It didn't work.

"Don't worry, honey," he said. "Your turn is comin'. I just have a little loose end to tie up below, and then you and I are gonna...talk." He smiled, his gaze flicking to her breasts and then back up to her face.

The gesture sent a chill down her spine. "I'd rather be dead." Heather all but spat the words.

His smiled faded as though it had never been. "Oh, don't worry. You will be. Eventually."

"Bastard!" Heather kicked him in the shin and tried to jerk her arm from his grasp.

Without warning, DiMona's fist shot out, catching her on the jaw. Heather fell hard. Dazed, barely conscious, she fought against the blackness that threatened to swamp her. Court needed her.

She stared blearily at DiMona's back as he shouted to Court again. "Come on out, Morgan. And maybe I'll let your girlfriend live." DiMona was ignoring her now, obviously not considering her to be a threat. Crawling, staying low to avoid attracting his attention, Heather began to work her way closer to him.

"That's it," DiMona yelled. And to her horror, Heather saw that Court, using the tree limb as a cane, was limping into the open.

"No! No! No!" she murmured, coming to her feet. Damn him and his selfless hero makeup. He seemed to be willing to let DiMona kill him on the off chance that doing so would save Heather's life.

"Let her go!" Court shouted from below. "She's no threat to you."

DiMona pretended to consider. "Nah, I can't do that." And then he lifted the rifle to sight down its barrel as he targeted Court.

The time for thinking was over. It was time for Heather to face her fear…and conquer it. Reacting instinctively, she jerked the handgun from the waistband of her jeans and stepped quickly forward to press the muzzle firmly beneath DiMona's jaw. He froze.

"Pull that trigger and you're dead in the next second. You got that?"

"Sure. Sure. I got it, little girl. Just take it easy. You wouldn't want that thing to go off accidentally."

"Wouldn't I?" She wasn't so certain of that herself. "Drop the gun." As he made a movement that startled her, she barked, "Slowly! Or this just might go off."

He slowly lowered the gun to the ground. "Okay little girl. You're in control. Now what?"

Heather glanced quickly down into the meadow. Where was Court? She stepped back from DiMona. "Move over there." She indicated the spot where she'd landed when he'd punched her. "Sit down."

DiMona sat. "I know all about you, Heather. I know what happened to you when you were younger. I know how much you hate guns."

"Shut up!" The darned gun was heavier than she'd expected, especially when she had to keep holding it out at arm's length. Without taking her eyes off DiMona, she shouted for Court. "Court, I've got him."

There was no response. Damn! Maybe he'd lost

consciousness from blood loss. If so, she was on her own and she'd better figure out what to do.

She bit the inside of her bottom lip thoughtfully. She needed to tie him up, but even if she'd had some rope she didn't want to risk getting close enough to him to him to disarm her. So, tying him up was out of the question.

"You're so frightened you're shaking, Heather," DiMona observed. "Why don't you put that gun down and admit that you haven't got it in you to kill me. You probably couldn't even hit me."

"Oh, I could hit you all right," she assured him as she stole another glance down into the meadow, seeking Court. Where *was* he?

Then DiMona made a swift and unexpected movement, drawing a small pistol from behind his back. Reacting instinctively, knowing that he planned to kill her, Heather fired. Her accuracy was perfect, hitting him right where she'd aimed, in the right shoulder. The bullet wound threw his aim off, and knocked him back so that his bullet whistled harmlessly by Heather's ear. Racing forward while he was still stunned, she kicked the small handgun he'd dropped out of his reach and then stepped back to a safe distance. Surprise flared in DiMona's cold, cold eyes as he gripped his wounded shoulder.

Adrenaline reaction pounded through Heather's veins. She could hear her pulse in her ears. Feel the trembling in her limbs. She gulped oxygen, trying to slow her frantic heartbeat.

"I see you've gotten over your fear," DiMona observed.

Numbed by the realization that she'd actually shot

another human being, Heather could only stare at him. The depths of her own paralysis stunned her, and she realized that she had never really believed herself capable of shooting another human being. Oh, she'd told herself she could do what was necessary, but she hadn't *really* believed in herself. She'd thought herself too weak, too dependent on others: counsellors, doctors, her fiancé.

Oh, she and Des had been alone for a long time now. But that was in the normal world. Deep down, she always believed that, if it came down to the crunch in a situation where she needed to be strong, she'd fail herself…and Des. Just as she had ten years ago. But now…now she'd surprised herself by being more capable than she'd ever dreamed possible. And deep down, where the fear of failure had always resided, she felt a burgeoning sense of confidence.

A groan from DiMona brought her out of her paralysis. It wasn't time to celebrate yet. Her nemesis, although in pain, was still very much alive. And, if she didn't do something quickly, he could very well find a way to exact his revenge on her. But, what to do without placing herself within his grasp?

"Heather! Heather, answer me damn it! Are you all right?" It was Court. He was alive! Conscious!

"I'm fine," she called, still not daring to take her eyes off of DiMona. "We're here."

A moment later, Court came limping up the path carrying his rifle and using the stout branch as a cane. He must have gotten to the horses. She studied him worriedly, dividing her attention carefully between DiMona and Court. "What about you?" she asked. "How are you doing?"

"I'll live a while longer," he assured her, studying her closely. "What's this?" He ran his fingertips gently over her jaw.

At his touch, Heather involuntarily jerked away. Then, seeing the anger flare in his eyes, she tried to minimize the issue. "Just a bruise," she said with a shrug. "It'll heal." She didn't want Court angry until they were out of this.

Court cast a scathing look at DiMona who was sitting watching them with a smirk on his face. "I'd like nothing better than to see you dead, DiMona. Just give me a reason."

DiMona eyed him coldly, but said nothing.

Court looked back at Heather. "I need to loosen this tourniquet for a moment. Watch him closely, okay? If he moves, shoot him." He eyed the blood staining DiMona's shoulder and smiled coldly. "Again." Then brushing tender fingers over Heather's uninjured cheek he asked, "Okay?"

What he was really asking was if she thought she could handle more. She nodded and murmured, "Okay."

Setting his rifle down at his side, Court sat down next to the handgun that she'd kicked away from DiMona and carefully loosened the tourniquet. "I brought the horses," he informed her. "They're at the foot of the path. And help's on the way."

She looked at him in surprise. "How—"

"The cell phone worked. It was a bit staticky, but it got through."

Relief flooded through her. They were going to make it!

* * *

Court's room at the hospital was bright and sunny. After hours with all of Court's family present, Heather and Court had finally been left alone. DiMona was in custody and being flown back to Seattle. Ernest had called to let Court know they'd found enough pictorial evidence in DiMona's safety deposit box—once they'd tracked it down—to ensure that DiMona never saw the light of day outside a prison wall again. And, although Court was still pale, the doctor had said that he would recover completely from the bullet wound to his leg and the loss of blood.

Heather firmly stroked her hands over Court's foot, soothing the muscles in a gentle massage designed to stimulate blood flow and the healing process. He groaned, and her hands stilled. "Did I hurt you?"

He shook his head and her hands resumed their action. "Damn, that feels good," he murmured.

Heather smiled. "It's supposed to." She paused and grew serious. She owed this man so much. "Des told me what you did for him. And, well, I wanted to say thank you."

Court shrugged. "I just put in a good word for him."

A pretty weighty *good word,* if Heather wasn't mistaken. "Well, community service here in Montana while he takes a job with Kenzie is a far sight better than a jail term. And it gives him a chance to turn his life around."

"Forget it!" Court said. "It was no problem." Since her gratitude seemed to make him uncomfortable, Heather fell silent.

But a moment later, it was Court who broke the silence. "Heather—"

Warned by the seriousness of his tone, Heather lifted her gaze to meet his. "Yes?"

"Remember…out there…when I said that I had something to tell you, too?"

She nodded.

He cleared his throat. "Well, do you recall me telling you that I was finally starting to feel more accepting of Carly's death? Less guilty about all the shouldas, wouldas, couldas?" Heather nodded, and he continued. "Well, I've been thinking for a while now about leaving the DEA and coming back to Montana. It's home, and I've missed it."

No longer able to meet his gaze, Heather looked out the window. He was trying to tell her that he was leaving Seattle and that he wouldn't be able to see her anymore. She swallowed and tried to focus on his words.

"Anyway, Chance says that the sheriff's position in Big Springs is coming up for reelection next month and that I'd be a shoo-in. Even if I don't get it though, Mom's been trying to get me to take over the northeast quarter for years."

Heather nodded, suppressing her own pain, focusing on what would be best for Court. "I think that's a great idea. It's easy to see that you're a wide-open-spaces type of person at heart. And I think you'd make a wonderful small-town sheriff."

"You're sure?" Court asked. "It won't bother you being married to a guy that carries a gun?"

"I'm not as bothered by guns as I was. I guess—" Heather's mouth froze in an open position as the

words Court had said finally sank in. She was left
openmouthed and speechless.

"Well?"

Heather closed her mouth. "Um…are you asking
me to marry you?"

Court frowned. "Well, of course I am. What in
blazes did you think I was talking about?"

Heather smiled. "Never mind. It's not important."

"So…will you?" he prompted, his expression beginning to take on a decidedly disgruntled cast.
"Can you handle being married to a small-town
sheriff?"

Heather considered the question with mock seriousness, despite the fact that her heart was racing
with happiness. Finally, she said, "Oh, yeah. I think
I can handle that just fine."

"You do?" Court seemed surprised.

"I do."

"Whew! That was way easier than I thought it
was going to be."

"Oh, well, in that case, perhaps I should think
about it a bit."

He grinned. "Too late. You're mine. Now come
here and let me kiss you properly."

Being careful not do jostle his leg, Heather complied. Happily.

* * * * *

If you enjoyed what you just read,
then we've got an offer you can't resist!

Take 2 bestselling love stories FREE!

Plus get a FREE surprise gift!

Look Who's Celebrating Our 20th Anniversary:

Celebrate
20
YEARS

"In 1980, Silhouette gave a home to my first book and became my family. Happy 20th Anniversary! And may we celebrate twenty more."

—*New York Times* bestselling author
Nora Roberts

"Twenty years of Silhouette! I can hardly believe it. Looking back on it, I find that my life and my books for Silhouette were inextricably intertwined.... Every Silhouette I wrote was a piece of my life. So, thank you, Silhouette, and may you have many more anniversaries."

—International bestselling author
Candace Camp

"Twenty years publishing fiction by women, for women, and about women is something to celebrate! I am honored to be a part of Silhouette's proud tradition— one that I have no doubt will continue being cherished by women the world over for a long, long time to come."

—International bestselling author
Maggie Shayne

SILHOUETTE'S 20TH ANNIVERSARY CONTEST
OFFICIAL RULES
NO PURCHASE NECESSARY TO ENTER

1. To enter, follow directions published in the offer to which you are responding. Contest begins 1/1/00 and ends on 8/24/00 (the "Promotion Period"). Method of entry may vary. Mailed entries must be postmarked by 8/24/00, and received by 8/31/00.

2. During the Promotion Period, the Contest may be presented via the Internet. Entry via the Internet may be restricted to residents of certain geographic areas that are disclosed on the Web site. To enter via the Internet, if you are a resident of a geographic area in which Internet entry is permissible, follow the directions displayed on-line, including typing your essay of 100 words or fewer telling us "Where In The World Your Love Will Come Alive." On-line entries must be received by 11:59 p.m. Eastern Standard time on 8/24/00. Limit one e-mail entry per person, household and e-mail address per day, per presentation. If you are a resident of a geographic area in which entry via the Internet is permissible, you may, in lieu of submitting an entry on-line, enter by mail, by hand-printing your name, address, telephone number and contest number/name on an 8"x 11" plain piece of paper and telling us in 100 words or fewer "Where In The World Your Love Will Come Alive," and mailing via first-class mail to: Silhouette 20th Anniversary Contest, (in the U.S.) P.O. Box 9069, Buffalo, NY 14269-9069; (In Canada) P.O. Box 637, Fort Erie, Ontario, Canada L2A 5X3. Limit one 8"x 11" mailed entry per person, household and e-mail address per day. On-line and/or 8"x 11" mailed entries received from persons residing in geographic areas in which Internet entry is not permissible will be disqualified. No liability is assumed for lost, late, incomplete, inaccurate, nondelivered or misdirected mail, or misdirected e-mail, for technical, hardware or software failures of any kind, lost or unavailable network connection, or failed, incomplete, garbled or delayed computer transmission or any human error which may occur in the receipt or processing of the entries in the contest.

3. Essays will be judged by a panel of members of the Silhouette editorial and marketing staff based on the following criteria:

   Sincerity (believability, credibility)—50%

   Originality (freshness, creativity)—30%

   Aptness (appropriateness to contest ideas)—20%

   Purchase or acceptance of a product offer does not improve your chances of winning. In the event of a tie, duplicate prizes will be awarded.

4. All entries become the property of Harlequin Enterprises Ltd., and will not be returned. Winner will be determined no later than 10/31/00 and will be notified by mail. Grand Prize winner will be required to sign and return Affidavit of Eligibility within 15 days of receipt of notification. Noncompliance within the time period may result in disqualification and an alternative winner may be selected. All municipal, provincial, federal, state and local laws and regulations apply. Contest open only to residents of the U.S. and Canada who are 18 years of age or older, and is void wherever prohibited by law. Internet entry is restricted solely to residents of those geographical areas in which Internet entry is permissible. Employees of Torstar Corp., their affiliates, agents and members of their immediate families are not eligible. Taxes on the prizes are the sole responsibility of winners. Entry and acceptance of any prize offered constitutes permission to use winner's name, photograph or other likeness for the purposes of advertising, trade and promotion on behalf of Torstar Corp. without further compensation to the winner, unless prohibited by law. Torstar Corp and D.L. Blair, Inc., their parents, affiliates and subsidiaries, are not responsible for errors in printing or electronic presentation of contest or entries. In the event of printing or other errors which may result in unintended prize values or duplication of prizes, all affected contest materials or entries shall be null and void. If for any reason the Internet portion of the contest is not capable of running as planned, including infection by computer virus, bugs, tampering, unauthorized intervention, fraud, technical failures, or any other causes beyond the control of Torstar Corp. which corrupt or affect the administration, secrecy, fairness, integrity or proper conduct of the contest, Torstar Corp. reserves the right, at its sole discretion, to disqualify any individual who tampers with the entry process and to cancel, terminate, modify or suspend the contest or the Internet portion thereof. In the event of a dispute regarding an on-line entry, the entry will be deemed submitted by the authorized holder of the e-mail account submitted at the time of entry. Authorized account holder is defined as the natural person who is assigned to an e-mail address by an Internet access provider, on-line service provider or other organization that is responsible for arranging e-mail address for the domain associated with the submitted e-mail address.

5. Prizes: Grand Prize—a $10,000 vacation to anywhere in the world. Travelers (at least one must be 18 years of age or older) or parent or guardian if one traveler is a minor, must sign and return a Release of Liability prior to departure. Travel must be completed by December 31, 2001, and is subject to space and accommodations availability. Two hundred (200) Second Prizes—a two-book limited edition autographed collector set from one of the Silhouette Anniversary authors: Nora Roberts, Diana Palmer, Linda Howard or Annette Broadrick (value $10.00 each set). All prizes are valued in U.S. dollars.

6. For a list of winners (available after 10/31/00), send a self-addressed, stamped envelope to: Harlequin Silhouette 20th Anniversary Winners, P.O. Box 4200, Blair, NE 68009-4200.

Contest sponsored by Torstar Corp., P.O. Box 9042, Buffalo, NY 14269-9042.

PS20RULES

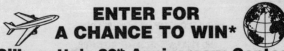

ENTER FOR
A CHANCE TO WIN*

Silhouette's 20th Anniversary Contest

Tell Us Where in the World
You Would Like *Your* Love To Come Alive...
And We'll Send the Lucky Winner There!

Silhouette wants to take you wherever
your happy ending can come true.

Here's how to enter: Tell us, in 100 words or less,
where you want to go to make your love come alive!

In addition to the grand prize, there will be 200
runner-up prizes, collector's-edition book sets
autographed by one of the Silhouette anniversary
authors: **Nora Roberts, Diana Palmer,
Linda Howard** or **Annette Broadrick**.

DON'T MISS YOUR CHANCE TO WIN!
ENTER NOW! No Purchase Necessary

Silhouette®
Where love comes alive™

Visit Silhouette at www.eHarlequin.com to enter, starting this summer.

Name:

Address:

City: State/Province:

Zip/Postal Code:

Mail to Harlequin Books: **In the U.S.**: P.O. Box 9069, Buffalo, NY
14269-9069; **In Canada**: P.O. Box 637, Fort Erie, Ontario, L4A 5X3

*No purchase necessary—for contest details send a self-addressed stamped envelope to:
Silhouette's 20th Anniversary Contest, P.O. Box 9069, Buffalo, NY, 14269-9069 (include
contest name on self-addressed envelope). Residents of Washington and Vermont may
omit postage. Open to Cdn. (excluding Quebec) and U.S. residents who are 18 or over.
Void where prohibited. Contest ends August 31, 2000.   PS20CON_R2